# SPY FORCE

## mission:
### *The Nightmare Vortex*

Look for all of the
**SPY FORCE**
adventures

**Coming soon**

# SPY

# FORCE

## mission:
### *The Nightmare Vortex*

**BY DEBORAH ABELA · ILLUSTRATED BY GEORGE O'CONNOR**

Paula Wiseman Book · Simon & Schuster Books for Young Readers
New York    London    Toronto    Sydney

SIMON & SCHUSTER BOOKS FOR YOUNG READERS
An imprint of Simon & Schuster Children's Publishing Division
1230 Avenue of the Americas, New York, New York 10020
Text copyright © 2003 by Deborah Abela
Illustrations copyright © 2005 by George O'Connor
Cover photograph copyright © Schafer & Hill/Getty Images
First published in Australia in 2003 by Random House Australia Pty Ltd
Published by arrangement with Random House Australia Pty Ltd
First illustrated U.S. edition, 2005
SIMON & SCHUSTER BOOKS FOR YOUNG READERS is a
trademark of Simon & Schuster, Inc.
Book design by Lucy Ruth Cummins
The text for this book is set in Goudy.
The illustrations for this book are rendered in ink.
Manufactured in the United States of America
10 9 8 7 6 5 4 3 2 1
CIP data for this book is available from the Library of Congress.
ISBN-13: 978-0-689-87359-1
ISBN-10: 0-689-87359-X

For Mr. and Mrs. Pozzi

# A LETTER FROM MAX REMY, SUPERSPY

A lot has happened since I saw you last. Remember how I wrote about the elite intelligence agency Spy Force and Alex Crane, who is their top spy? Well, it's true! Spy Force actually exists and not only that, after hearing about Linden and me in action as a dynamic spy duo during our last mission with the Matter Transporter, Spy Force invited us to become their youngest secret agents. How about that? We are official, world-class spies.

We visited Spy Force Headquarters in London, and it's full of amazing vehicles like the hyperfast Invisible Jet, gadgets like the Slimer and the Stinkbomb, and the smartest agents and inventors in the world. Except for Dretch, a former agent who's really mean and I think is planning to get rid of us as soon as he gets the chance. I'm staying away from him.

We also went on our first official mission.

The evil Mr. Blue had set up a food factory and was planning to put a mind-control ingredient in kids' food that would turn them into his loyal followers, but there was no danger of that happening with Linden and me on the case. Oh, and we got a little help from that Goody Two-shoes Ella. You remember her? The one Linden thinks is SOOO funny.

We entered the factory disguised as BRATTs — Bona Fide Authorized Taste Testers — and our mission was to discover where the ingredient was and destroy it before Blue could use it. Blue is pretty smart and he managed to slip Linden some of the secret ingredient, and it looked like he was going to double-cross us and leave us to meet our fate in the Moons of Mars confectionary room, but the ingredient wore off and he saved us before Ella and I were carved up into little cookie pieces.

Anyway, there are lots of other details about the mission, but I have to get going. It looks like Blue's up to something else dastardly, and no doubt it will be up to Linden and me to save the world again.

Signing off from Secret Agent Max Remy, Superspy.

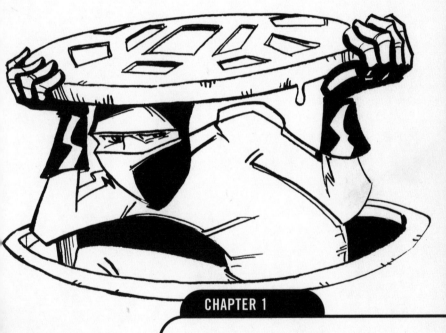

**CHAPTER 1**

# A Mysterious Happening

**Chronicles of Spy Force:**

It all started within the secret underground fortress deep in the subterranean labyrinth of Spy Force. Reinforced with ten-feet-thick cement walls poured around indestructible beams of titanium, the fortress had a laser-sensitive surface that detected and dealt with unwelcome elements in an instant.

This was one of the most important areas of the Force.

It was the mail room.

No mail entered or left the building without passing through the highly trained hands of an elite team of postage handlers and deliverers, equipped with the nerves and skills to make them unbreakable to all enemies of the Force. In the spy game if information falls into the wrong hands, the fate of the entire agency, even the world, could be at stake.

Two small unassuming parcels entered the X-ray machine. The small *y* inscribed in invisible ink and detected by the rays meant they were from Harrison, chief of Spy Force, and were bound for two new spies. The packages were cleared and sent through a whirling maze of conveyor belts that zigzagged around the high-security operation to the delivery van of Agent Z11.

Agent Z11 started the van. Like on any other day, she'd completed a thorough inspection of the vehicle. Everything checked. Gaining clearance from High Command to leave the building, Agent Z11 made her way out of the building through a secret network of underground alleys until she reached a quiet suburban street and was on her way.

Agent Z11 whistled as she drove, oblivious as to what was to happen next.

On entering a long, underground tunnel, traffic came to a standstill. A police officer approached her van and told her there'd been a breakdown. Road and Safety tow trucks were on their way. She checked her watch. Agent Z11 didn't like being interrupted in carrying out Spy Force business.

Just then, the lights went out. An eerie glow filled the tunnel as headlights provided the only source of light.

Agent Z11 tried not to think of the valuable seconds she was losing. She had never, in seven years, failed to deliver a package on time.

Up ahead two drivers got out of their cars and started yelling at each other. More drivers got out as the argument became heated. Agent Z11 stayed where she was. Her priority was her cargo, not two hotheads losing it in a traffic jam.

Agent Z11 got out of the van, locked the doors, and circled the vehicle with her flashlight. Nothing had been touched. Nothing had been tampered with.

Below the tunnel, in a large, smelly, rat-infested river of slime that ran through the city's sewers, a man dressed in black with a mask and gloves lifted a steel manhole cover and aimed a silent laser beam up into the thick metal floor of a van. Within minutes he lifted himself out of the sewer and into the van of Agent Z11. With an infrared microflashlight set in the side of his glasses, he sifted through the packages, discarding most, until he found what he was looking for.

A small unassuming package addressed to Max Remy.

Agent Z11 rolled her eyes as the arguing drivers began shoving each other. She checked her watch again before doing another round of the van. Each second that passed was making her more and more uneasy.

Using a special heat ray to unstick the glue, the masked man opened the parcel for Max Remy and removed a small badge, replaced it with a seemingly identical one. Almost as fast, he resealed the package, before carefully lowering himself back down into the sewer, welding the bottom of the van closed, so that even he had trouble noticing the intrusion.

Suddenly the lights came on in the tunnel. The manhole cover was slipped quietly back into place. The two hotheads calmed down and drivers returned to their vehicles as the broken-down car was towed away.

*Finally*, thought Agent Z11. *I can make up for lost time on the freeway.*

She started her van as, deep within the city's sewers, a masked man dressed in black splashed through the filthy green-brown slime to make a quick and unseen getaway.

CHAPTER 2

Be Careful Where
You Step

Max walked home from school with her notebook in hand and her eyes darting over the city like searchlights. There were suspicious people everywhere hopelessly entangled in a web of dubious activities, and now that she and Linden were full-fledged spies, it was up to her to take note of it all.

She opened the cover of her red chrome Spy Force microrecorder watch.

"3:30 P.M. New York, New York. Agent Max Remy signing in. Each second of every day there are strange and mysterious happenings all around us that only the well-trained eye can see. A good spy will always be on their toes and always be careful where they step."

Just then, reflected in a shop window, Max saw a car racing straight toward her. She leaped out of the way at lightning speed, landing against a nearby wall and only narrowly avoiding the splash of water from the gutter.

"Trouble may be just behind you." She looked over her shoulder and walked on. "And a special agent must always be on the lookout for where it might lie. . . . Aaaahhh!"

"Foofff!"

Max opened her eyes to see the world was the wrong way round and it was full of . . . colored feathers.

"Hey. Are you okay?"

Max shook her head. "Ah. I think so. What happened?"

A tubby, bald man looked down on her.

"You tumbled into this crate of feathers we're taking

into the theater. With skills like that, little girl, you could join the circus."

Circus? Little girl? She was an international spy who had saved the world. Twice.

"Could you just help me out of here?" But as she said this, a tall, skinny guy wearing a pair of oversize overalls tripped up the curb, sending his bucket of pink goop sprawling into the air. Max looked up and saw the whole thing in slow motion, just seconds before she was transformed into a giant feathered, sticky mess.

"I . . . gee . . . sorry about—" the guy started to apologize, but Max interrupted.

"Just get me out."

After the two men helped her out, Max fumed as she made her feathered way home, thinking now might be a good time to move out and avoid another of her mother's screaming attacks about how clumsy she was.

As she opened the front door of her home, she heard her mother talking to her freak-fashioned boyfriend, Aidan. Max could not let either of them see her like this and, quietly sneaking behind them, she tiptoed upstairs to her bedroom and locked the door behind her.

*Phew!* Max sighed as she leaned against the door, but just when she thought she was safe, her mother tried to force her way in.

"Sweetie? Open up, I want to tell you something."

Max desperately tried to get undressed, but the goo

and feathers had stiffened and her clothes wouldn't budge. Her mother was still calming down about an expensive Persian rug Max had spilled a strawberry smoothie on. If her mom saw her like this, she'd be grounded for life.

"Tell me from there. I'm studying and I don't want to lose concentration."

Just like knocking, accepting "no" for an answer was something her mother never did. "Open this door now."

Max searched the room for something that would save her life. "Coming."

The door opened. Max's mother entered and looked around.

"Are you hiding something?"

"No." Max wore a towel around her head and was draped in a long bathrobe. Her mother didn't seem convinced but made herself at home on Max's bed and began.

"We're having a party here to welcome a few new personalities to the network."

A party! Suddenly being covered in pink goop and feathers hardly mattered at all.

"We want to make them feel like part of a family and to get everyone friendlier with each other."

Max's stony face stared. Great! They want to get friendly while I get invaded in my own home. But then she was struck by a thought. She'd asked if Linden could visit and didn't want to do anything that might jeopardize that.

"That'll be fun." She tried to sound genuine. "What about Linden?"

"Who?" Her mom rarely remembered things that had nothing to do with her.

"Linden. My friend from Pennsylvania. He's coming to stay for a week. You even signed a form saying you'll look after him while he goes to my school."

"Oh. When's he coming?" Max's mom stood up and walked toward the door.

"Tomorrow. You were going to arrange it with his dad. Remember?"

"I'll call him tonight. I promise." And with that she left the room.

"But . . ." Max hurried after her but rebounded off a mountain of boxes blocking her way and fell to the floor.

Bathroom stuff fell everywhere. Shampoos, conditioners, body wash, cologne. Stacks of it. Max looked up. It was Aidan. Each day he was getting more and more comfortable in their house and now it seemed he was moving in!

Max was furious, but she couldn't think about Aidan right now. Her towel had wriggled off her head and her mother's face was twisting into an expression of maximum anger.

"What on earth have you . . . ?"

Max tried to explain what had happened, but it did no good. Her mother filled the next few minutes of Max's life shrieking about how she had the clumsiest daughter in the world.

She also, as always, had the last word. "If you want your little friend to stay, you'll have to be very careful where you step, young lady."

Max hated when she called her that. First, she never wanted to be a lady. It was so girly. And second, whenever she was called "young lady," it meant if she did anything wrong over the next few days, she could kiss any chance of happiness good-bye for a very long time.

Max got off the floor and walked into the bathroom to start washing her feathered outfit away. She was so angry but knew if she wanted Linden to stay, she'd have to do everything her mother's way. Which included pretending to like Aidan.

"And I thought saving the world was hard," she muttered. "Pretending to like Aidan is going to make this one of the hardest weeks of my life."

**CHAPTER 3**

A Country Visitor and
News About the Time
and Space Machine

**Chronicles of Spy Force:**

Superspy Max Remy slammed her pick into the side of Popocatepetl in Mexico, a volcano that rose almost fourteen thousand feet above sea level to a snow-covered, blue-sky summit. She was climbing to the top in an attempt to infiltrate the secret hideout of Count Blackheart, one of the world's deadliest fiends. Closely behind her was Alex Crane. The two spies were the best in the business and since becoming partners, were also inseparable friends.

"Max? How long until we reach the top?"

Max brushed snow from her goggles and saw their destination a few yards above. "About thirty minutes."

"Good. My foot's got this itch I'm dying to scratch."

The two laughed until the hook securing Alex's rope snapped and she swung away from the cliff with nothing more than Max for support.

"Alex!" Max reached out to her friend, but the wind buffeted her away. She loosened her rope to reach farther, but it was no good. Alex fluttered like a burst hot air balloon battered by the icy winds.

Max had another plan, but just as she was about to try it, a helicopter swung over the edge of the summit, whipping the snow into a blinding storm and the winds into an even greater frenzy. A man carrying a large shiny knife was lowered on a long, metal cable.

"Farewell, ladies." Blackheart's voice reverberated from a loudspeaker.

Max needed to think fast. She had to get to Alex before the knife-wielding man did and before the force of the helicopter tore them both off the mountain. Before . . .

"Max!"

Max's head spun round. She wasn't climbing the summit of Popocatepetl. She was in her room, and that was the sound of her mother calling.

The door opened. Why didn't her mother ever knock?

"There's a package for you. It's from overseas." She handed it to Max and stood there waiting for her to open it. Max put it on her bed and kept typing.

"Thanks. I'll open it later. It's probably something from Dad," Max said, trying to put her mother off.

"Don't you want to see what it is?" asked her mother, curious to see who the package was from.

"Yeah. I just want to finish this first."

"Okay, sweetie. I'll be downstairs."

After her dad had left them for his new actress wife, Max's mother hadn't mentioned his name once. It was a kind of rule between them, but Max knew that didn't mean she didn't want to know what he was up to.

When her mother was far enough away, Max locked the door and opened the package. It wasn't from her dad, it was from Spy Force. She picked up a small handheld device. The screen lit up and a soft voice spoke.

"Max Remy fingerprint identification complete. And now a word from our leader."

Harrison's face appeared on the screen. He had a bandage around his head and a whiplash collar on his neck. Next to Harrison, Max didn't seem clumsy at all.

"Hello, Max. How are you? Of course you can't answer me, this is a recording. Don't mind the bandages. A little accident with a hair dryer and a food processor.

"This parcel has some things you'll need over the next few days. I'm talking to you from a palm computer. Yours is enclosed. The best, most secure way to contact other rangers . . . I mean, *agents*. It also has a complete library of Spy Force literature with Internet access for updates. You'll find *A Brief History of Spy Force*, which tells of the beginnings of the agency and has a few favorite recipes as well. There's also *The Guide to Spy Force Missions*, subtitled, *How They Did It*, which lists every Spy Force mission ever completed. There's a training manual to read for your exam and finally, the secret badge of Spy Force. Steinberger will be in frogfat . . . that is, *contact*, to tell you more. Linden is receiving the same material. Remember, if you download anything, it must be destroyed. All Spy Force material is top secret.

"Snood fie . . . Oh golly, I mean, good-bye."

Max opened *The Guide to Spy Force Missions* and looked up Alex's name. She watched as full-color pictures showed

17

Alex rappelling in the Andes, diving in the Mediterranean, and hiding in the markets of Marrakesh, Morocco. She'd outwitted bad guys from Budapest to Boston, but not only that, Alex's father had been a spy too and they'd completed lots of missions together as Spy Force's only father-and-daughter team. Max flinched. She's seen this picture somewhere before, but where and why? She scrabbled through her brain to figure out how she could have seen it when it was in a top-secret file she was seeing for the first time. But before she could think about it any further, she saw something else. One mission had been deleted. When Max opened the page, it was blank.

"What happened here?"

Max's alarm went off. She'd set it to remind her to check if her mom had called Linden's dad. She put the palm computer away, slipped the secret badge in her pocket, and went downstairs.

Her mom was in full flight organizing the "personality" party with a horde of people running after her every whim.

*That's it!* decided Max. If her mother wasn't going to make the call, she'd do it for her.

"Mom!" she yelled over the noise. "It's Linden's dad on the phone."

Max held out the receiver while her mother gave her a "You're in trouble" look, but then was sweet as pie when she said "hello." Max listened as everything was arranged. "So we'll expect the arrival of . . . of . . ."

"Linden!" Max whispered in horror.

". . . of Linden this afternoon. Good-bye." She flounced her hair. "Linden's dad sounds nice. Very mature."

At that moment Aidan bounced up holding a doll that looked suspiciously like him. "Look at this."

"What is it?" Max cringed.

"It's a Rex doll. After my character on the show." He'd been given the role of a psychologist on a new soap.

Max did her best not to throw up.

"I'll be upstairs."

Max did all she could over the next few hours to block out the noise from downstairs until she finally saw her uncle Ben and his brother, Francis, pull up outside her apartment building. They were brilliant scientists and would be in the city all week for meetings and had offered to give Linden a lift. Max jumped off her bed and raced downstairs.

"They're here," she yelled as she flew past her mom.

"Who?"

Max opened the door and saw the beaming face and wild hair of Linden staring back at her. She was so happy to see him, she almost reached out and hugged him until she realized what she was about to do and stopped herself just in time.

Her mom walked up behind her like she'd recently been made queen of somewhere, and put on one of her best acts of snobbiness.

"Well, if it isn't our country friends," she said over-loudly. "And . . . and . . ."

Max swung her head round to face her mother. "Linden!" she whispered.

"Yes. You'll be in the spare room," her mom said, but did nothing more to invite them in, so they all stood in an awkward silence that made Max burn up with embarrassment until Ben rescued them.

"We thought we'd take the kids out for dinner, if that's all right with you."

Everyone sighed, especially Max's mom. "That'd be lovely." And she slobbered a good-bye kiss over Max, who felt like she was drowning in saliva and lipstick.

"Are you sure you two are related?" Linden asked after they'd left.

"That's what it says on my birth certificate." Max sighed, but Linden's smile made her feel instantly better.

In the car they chatted wildly like there wasn't enough time in the world to talk about all their news, but mostly they talked about their Spy Force packages.

"Maybe they'll want us to go on another mission."

"Yeah! That's what I was thinking."

Ben had chosen a vegetarian restaurant just for Max, and after they'd finished eating, he clasped his hands together, and leaned toward them excitedly.

"Now, we have something to tell you."

Max waited anxiously as Linden struggled with the wrapper of an after-dinner mint the waiter had just left.

"Francis and I have finished the Time and Space Machine."

"Finished the Time and Space Machine!" Max yelled as they tried to shush her.

"I think it's supposed to be a secret," Linden mumbled through a chocolate-covered mouth.

"Sorry."

Ben explained how they did it, including how they'd added the Time and Space Retractor Meter that Linden and Max had helped bring to America from London.* "But the key component to the new Time and Space Machine was Francis's discovery."

Ben wiped his napkin across his mouth. "Want to come to the lab and see?"

"In Pennsylvania?" Max was confused.

"No. We've got one here." Ben kept his voice lowered.

"Yeah, but it's a little more advanced than the shed." Francis smiled.

Linden and Max leaped out of their seats and raced to the car. The journey to the lab seemed to take forever. Finally, they drove up to two security guards standing by tall metal gates.

Francis pulled out a pass like he was some kind of FBI agent. "They're with me," he said proudly.

*See *Mission: In Search of the Time and Space Machine.*

"Certainly, Professors." The guards stood aside and opened the gates. Max was impressed. This was very different from how Francis had been treated in London.

Inside the entrance, two lab assistants helped Max and Linden into white sanitized suits, shower caps, and balloon-like shoe covers.

"What do you think?" Linden asked Max. "Does it say, chick magnet?"

"I'm surprised you haven't been mobbed already."

"I don't know," whispered Francis. "I thought one of the lab assistants was looking at you funny."

"Mom always said I'd be a winner with the girls."

Ben and Max giggled at Linden's attempt to look suave, before heading off through a series of security doors and ultrawhite passages. They then stepped into a foyer-type room in front of the lab.

"The temperature in the lab is rigorously monitored," Francis began. "This room reads our collective temperature and adjusts the lab's temp accordingly. Once that is done, a release valve will be activated and we can go inside."

After a few more seconds, a metallic click was heard and they entered the lab.

Francis was right. It was a lot better than Ben's shed. There were shiny machines, with tubes, gadgets, and gizmos everywhere.

"Now, to the secret component." Francis looked so happy surrounded by scientific equipment.

He opened a small glass cabinet and removed a deep-blue velvet cloth. After carefully unfolding it, he placed it on a bench before them. "Here it is."

Max and Linden stared. "A rock?"

"Not just any rock," Ben interrupted excitedly. "Tell them, Francis."

Francis dimmed the lights with a remote. "Now look."

"Wow," Max and Linden breathed together. Inside the rock were swirling patches of colored light.

"It's like the auroras borealis and australis." Linden had seen pictures of the light phenomena but had never seen them for real.

"That's right. After I left the Department of Science and New Technologies, I was so sad at what had happened, I just went walking. I walked all over the United Kingdom, until I came across a little town in Scotland where the locals talked about these rocks called Aurora Stones. When I saw them, I knew they were special and have kept one with me ever since. It was in my pocket the day I met you. When I arrived in Pennsylvania, your aunt Eleanor helped me analyze it and we found it had a very special energy source. I've heard scientists talk about the stone, but no one knew for certain if it really existed."

Francis's eyes were alive with his discovery.

"When Ben and I experimented with using it in the Time and Space Machine, we found it gave us the missing energy source needed to move at the speed of light, thus enabling time travel."

Max and Linden stared at the rock as it glowed before them.

"When can we see the Time and Space Machine?"

Ben turned to Francis with a knowing smile. "I'd say any day now, but you'll have to be patient."

Linden's eyebrows sprang upward. "This is Max you're talking about. Patience isn't something she's spent a lot of time developing."

"I can be patient." Max folded her arms across her chest, glaring at Linden.

After about thirty seconds, she couldn't stand it. "How *long* do we have to wait?"

"When it's done, you'll know," Ben said. "For now, we better get you home and get on our way back to the farm."

Francis rewrapped the stone and locked it securely away as Max and Linden fired off an endless stream of questions about the new Time and Space Machine. Meanwhile, on the other side of the world, a man smiled maliciously as he listened to the sound of voices transmitting all the way from New York.

CHAPTER 4

The Personality
Party and a
Strange Guest

Linden and Max stepped out of their bedrooms and stood against the railing looking down on the final party preparations. The apartment had been completely transformed into a Japanese-style garden. There were bonsai plants, trickling water features, expensive vases and lamps, and meandering paths of white glistening rocks.

Linden ducked as a giant tree swooped past. "Is it always like this around here?"

"Only when I'm being punished," Max replied. "There's a party here tonight for Mom's TV types, which means the house will be full of people talking and laughing about boring things that aren't funny."

"Sounds great." Linden groaned.

"It'll be the night of my life," Max said dryly. "Breakfast?"

Linden and Max went downstairs and only narrowly avoided being swallowed up by a tidal wave of tablecloths.

"The blue," said Max's mom over the rim of her glasses. "No. Red. Shows we're in charge but warm at the same time. Ah, there you are, sweeties. Did you sleep well?"

Linden started to answer, but Max's mother interrupted. "Help yourself to breakfast. Mind you, don't step on that rug. I want it fresh for tonight. I had it brought in from Turkey."

She saw a furniture man placing a giant vase on the marble floor. "No, no, no . . . not there. Over there."

Max sighed. "That's another thing about my mom.

When she asks a question, she rarely waits around for an answer."

They grabbed some juice and toast and made their way back to Max's room, where they found a message light flashing on her palm computer.

"Hello, Max and Linden. Ben and Francis said you'd be there. How are you?"

It was Steinberger. Max and Linden waited for the rest of his message.

"This isn't a recording. I'm live. You can answer."

"Excellent," Linden muttered through his toast.

"Now that you've received your packages, the next step is spy training, which starts tomorrow and will continue all week after school. The training manual will explain what you'll be doing and what you'll need for the exam at the end."

"Where will we train?"

"In the Spy Force office in New York."

"In New York?"

"Yes, Max. Actually, it's right near your home. We'll provide a cover for you by saying there'll be sports at school every night this week as part of a kids' fitness campaign and . . . oh, you'll be trained by one of our best."

Max jumped off her bed. "Alex?"

"No." Steinberger sensed her disappointment. "But someone just as good."

"Will we be sent on another mission soon?"

"Not yet, Linden. You'll be busy with your training for a while. Ben and Francis will pick you up tomorrow morning at nine for your first session. Good luck and may the Force be with you."

Steinberger zapped off the screen.

Max and Linden spent the rest of the afternoon studying their training manuals until Max's mother burst through the door looking like an oversize swan with a hairdo like a small tornado had whizzed through it.

Max stared. "What are you wearing?"

"Do you like it? It's designer. Very expensive. The only one of its kind in the world. Anyway, time to get dressed. Linden, do you have something you can wear?"

"I was going to wear this." Linden looked down at his clothes. It was his best outfit. His dad had made him pack it especially.

"Fine." She wasn't sure what else to say. "There are plenty of combs in the bathroom too. You've certainly got a lot of hair for a small boy." Max's mom looked at Linden's hair like it was a wild animal she wanted to send to the beauty parlor for taming. "I'll see you downstairs."

It was times like these Max wished she was an orphan. "Sorry. She doesn't have much tact sometimes."

"It's not her fault she can't recognize style when she sees it." Linden tousled his hair and made it stand out even further.

Max smiled. Linden was her only chance of making it through the night.

They went downstairs and made their way through the overdressed crowd of people talking so loudly it was like they were in the middle of a storm. Everyone was "darling this" or "darling that" except for the guy who was hoarding food like he hadn't eaten in a million years. And what's more, almost all of them were smoking!

"Haven't they listened to a health report since the sixties?" Max walked away as someone blew smoke in her face. "News flash, everyone: Smoking can kill you. Everyone born this side of the twenty-first century knows that."

Stiff-faced waiters came by with what Max and Linden thought was food.

Linden went to take some.

"I wouldn't if I were you," Max cautioned. "Could be anything."

"But I'm starving." He picked up a small piece and took a bite. "What is it?" he asked the waiter.

"Sautéed Venezuelan slugs on a bed of tripe."

Linden stopped chewing. "Slugs on cow's stomach?"

"We prefer to call it tripe," the waiter snipped, and turned away.

"Maybe not eating for one night won't hurt me," Linden said, feeling queasy.

"Oh no," Max moaned. "There's a movie star wannabe coming our way."

She tried to make a getaway but was too late.

"Max! Hi. How lovely to see you. Is this your boyfriend?"

Max felt her face fire up like she'd been dropped into a furnace. "He's a friend."

"Oh. Did you see me in *Snow Ponies*? What did you think? It won't be long until I get snapped up for the movies or become a pop star. That's where the big dollars are."

If Max had to listen to any more of this drivel her insides were going to explode over everyone. "I think I heard my mom calling."

"Say hello to her for me!" the actress said as Max and Linden wriggled away.

"Remind me never to be like these people," Max said decisively.

"That'd only happen if your brain was removed and replaced with a slightly damp sponge."

Max smiled.

"Hey," Linden said excitedly. "I think that looks like bread."

He grabbed a roll from a passing waiter as Max spotted Aidan in full schmooze mode with the head of the network.

"Look."

She nudged Linden and pointed to a bowl of dip directly beneath Aidan's arm and just as he gave one of those loud fake laughs, he leaned right into it. When he pulled his hand up, the bowl of dip came with it and landed all over the shirt of the network boss. Max and Linden laughed as Aidan apologized and tried to wipe off the big fishy globs, which made the mess even worse.

"Good to see you two enjoying yourselves." It was Max's mother, who hadn't yet noticed Aidan's dilemma.

Max's laugh was cut short when she noticed a man unlike all the other guests, staring at her intently.

"Mom? Who's that guy there?" But as she asked this, the man disappeared behind a large plant.

"I'm not sure, sweetie. Probably a hanger-on. Television is so full of them. Have you had enough to eat?" Before they could answer, she was called away. "I have to go, darling. Work is calling."

"Did you see him?" Max asked Linden, trying to see where the man went. "He was real weird-looking."

"He'd fit right in then, wouldn't he?"

Maybe he was just a hanger-on like her mother said, but there was something about the way he was staring at her that made Max feel uneasy, like he was up to something and it included her.

"How about we make a quick getaway?"

"Fine by me," said Linden, still trying to find a tray of recognizable food.

Max snuck along the hall, grabbing the phone on the way. "Takeout?"

Linden's fears of dying from hunger faded. "You bet."

They quickly ran upstairs to the safety of Max's room, as the man who had been staring at her followed them into the hall, his eyes fixed on their every step as he pulled a radio transceiver from his pocket.

"Not long now, boss, and you'll have exactly what you want."

**CHAPTER 5**

A Message from
Steinberger and a
Surprise Spy Trainer

**Chronicles of Spy Force:**

Alex Crane crouched among the bulging lines of cargo spilling across the wharves of the Grand Harbor in the Mediterranean country of Malta. The sun seared its way through a ninety-degree day as muscled men in sweat-soaked clothes sang and unloaded crates from hulks of ships that huddled like roped and captured giants.

The boats had sailed from Egypt, and when Alex adjusted the focus on her X-ray microfilm binoculars, she knew her hunch was right. The crates were brimming with stolen treasures from the ancient world.

She switched her binoculars from X-ray to regular to locate the sniveling Count Templar, the man with the fiendish taste for rare artifacts. He was sitting on a balcony with Max Remy, who was in disguise as a Transylvanian duchess eager to spend vast sums of money on the Count's wares. With Alex's microfilm and Max's deal, the Count would be locked away for so long that he himself would become an ancient artifact.

Alex looked at her watch. Max should have finished by now. She put on her supersonic earpiece and discovered the count had finished the deal but also wanted something else.

"You," Alex heard.

"Me?" Max was horrified. "For what?"

"Marriage." He almost growled.

*Marriage!* Alex watched as Max tried to evade the count's slimy moves and his wandering arms and lips that were fish-gulping, begging for a kiss. Alex knew she had to save her, but as she leaped forward, the cord of her binoculars snagged under her foot and she tripped, landing face first at the feet of the muscled men.

Her arms were pinned against her as the men lifted her into the air like a small, tattered doll, before striding to the dock and dangling her over the side, just seconds away from a watery doom. What was she going to do? She had to escape these muscle-bound men before it was too late . . . before she drowned and before Max became a victim of the Count's slobbering, lip-smacking . . .

*Brrrrrnnnnngggg!*

Max sat up clutching her pillow and gasping for breath.

"You okay?"

It took her a few seconds to take everything in. Linden was sitting on her bed holding the palm computer. She was in her pajamas. Then she remembered. Today was the day they would start their spy training.

Max was miffed that Linden was awake and she was half asleep with dreams of not quite saving the world.

"How long have you been there?"

"About five minutes."

"What if I wasn't decent?"

"I figured you would be since you said 'come in' when I knocked. It's all right." Linden looked around. "It'll be our little secret that you're not always perfectly dressed."

"That's not the point." Max began, trying to focus her sleepy eyes that were refusing to open. But it was exactly the point only, of course, she couldn't tell him that.

"Steinberger's waiting." Linden pointed to the palm computer.

"Already?" Max looked at her creased pajamas and pushed her ruffled hair out of her eyes. "Lucky those things see only one way."

"Oh no, I can see you quite well." Steinberger smiled. Max drooped. "Ready for your first dose of spy training?"

Linden's eyes widened. "Sure am!"

"Most of being a good spy is instinct, but there's also fitness and agility and that's what we'll concentrate on this weekend. Ah, I remember my first spy training when . . ."

Steinberger rambled on about his early days at Spy Force, while Max sat in quiet horror knowing fitness and agility were things her uncoordinated limbs knew nothing about.

Eventually, Steinberger wrapped up his story and wished them luck. "And may the Force be with you."

Max switched off the computer without hearing Steinberger's farewell. Putting her body through fitness and agility training was going to be like signing up for a trip to a medieval torture chamber.

Linden wondered where the look of terror on Max's face had come from. "Max?"

"Yeah?"

"You better get dressed. Ben and Francis'll be here soon."

"I know." She tried to look normal again. "I was just hoping getting dressed alone wasn't too much to ask."

"Oh," Linden said, a little embarrassed. "I'll be outside."

Downstairs, both Max's mom and the house looked immaculate. Aidan, however, looked terrible.

"Morning, Aidan." Max crunched her toast loudly in his ear. "Great party."

"Yeah," Aidan whispered, grabbing his head and covering his ears at the sound of the doorbell.

"That'll be Ben and Francis. Bye, Mom." She grabbed her bag and tried to escape before she fell victim to another of her mom's kisses, but it was too late. The kiss slobbered all over her.

Once they were outside, Max wiped her face against her sleeve. "She'll wear my face out if this goes on any longer."

"I'm sure she'll buy you a new one," Linden joked as they walked down the stairs. "Even though I like the old one."

Max fixed her eyes on Linden's face as her ears buzzed with what he'd just said, but with all that Linden-concentrating, she forgot to look where she was walking

40

and tumbled down the rest of the stairs.

"Aaaaaahhhh!"

When she landed at the bottom, Ben lifted her up and plunked her upright again.

"Didn't know you'd be so excited to see us, Max. Okay, everybody in the car."

While Linden sat watching the sights of New York, Max heard his words over and over again. She examined her face in the rearview mirror. She had a plain face. Her mother even said so. So how could Linden like it?

The car soon pulled up in front of a very regular-looking glass building in a very regular-looking street. It was four storys tall with double doors and not a sign anywhere saying what it was.

"You kids have a great time and remember, don't expect to be experts on your first day. Training can be tough." Ben ruffled Linden's hair and winked at Max. "Francis and I will be at the lab, and we'll pick you up at five."

Inside the building, a small woman with a pink cotton candy hairdo sat behind a desk.

"I'm Marion. Such a privilege to meet you. You're very famous, you know . . . in that quiet, spy world kind of way. But I won't keep you. Place your palms here and you'll be away."

Max and Linden pressed their hands onto a square plastic plate that lit up like a flattened Christmas tree.

After a few seconds a musical voice chimed, "Verification complete."

Marion's lips slooshed into a ear-creasing smile. "I knew you'd pass. It's through those doors. Good luck."

"Thanks," Linden said, amazed by the amount of smile Marion could fit onto her face. When they turned and entered the doors, they found themselves in a gymnasium with the usual ropes and trapezes hanging from the ceiling, treadmills, and rock-climbing walls, but also all sorts of bleeping, revolving devices and chambers they'd never seen before. Nestled among all the equipment was someone standing with their back to them.

"Excuse me. We're here for training," Max croaked nervously.

"You're three minutes late," the trainer said without turning around.

Linden looked at Max. *Oops*, he mouthed, but Max recognized the voice.

"Alex?"

The trainer turned around, her eyes fixed on her palm computer. It was Alex.

"I want fifty jumping jacks, twenty minutes on the treadmill, and fifty sit-ups."

Max's heart went into warp speed at seeing her hero. "Steinberger told us our trainer would be someone else."

"Well, you've got me. There's a bad case of flu going around and there was no one else to do it." Alex said, looking up for the first time since they'd arrived. "Well, what are you waiting for?"

Max and Linden dropped their bags and began jumping.

Max whispered to Linden, "It's Alex!"

"She doesn't seem too happy to see us."

"She's just being professional."

Max's fears of being uncoordinated came crashingly true as she fell from monkey bars, bounced off gym balls, collapsed into foam pits from swinging trapezes, and winded herself trying to clear pommel horses. Hard balls knocked her off her feet, and rope nets strung across giant rubber mattresses got her hopelessly tangled.

"Oooooph!" After several hours of Alex's rigorous training routine, Max fell from the rock-climbing wall and thudded onto a gym mat right at Alex's feet. Alex's head was buried in her computer as Linden landed expertly beside her.

"What's next?" he asked excitedly. Linden, of course, was good at all this stuff.

"The virtual cascades," Alex said, stepping over a flattened Max.

The two moved off as Max picked herself up.

"Don't worry about me. I'll be fine," she mumbled as she followed them into a darkened room and up onto a wooden platform.

"This is the virtual reality chamber," Alex began. "The next task must be completed wearing these specially-designed headsets."

Max and Linden took this as their cue to put the headsets on and when they did, what they saw was eye-popping. They weren't standing on a wooden platform anymore but on one side of a towering cliff top with a raging flood of water flowing beneath them.

Max was afraid of heights and even though she knew the waterfall wasn't real, she had to warn her legs to stop shaking.

"The headsets allow you to experience dangerous situations within the safety of the training center," Alex began. "Beside you is a Rappeller—a pocket-size device that allows you to descend heights or cross seemingly impassable distances. The Rappeller is fitted with a rope made of Venus flytrap fibers, which makes it extremely adhesive. Simply take hold of the rope, attach it to the wall behind us, and hurl the Rappeller toward the opposite cliff face, where it will adhere with an unbreakable strength. Climb along the rope to your destination, press the release button to disengage the fibers, and the Rappeller will retract. Any questions?"

Linden shook his head while Max concentrated on not passing out.

"Good. Before you is a chasm where the bridge has been blown out. You must use your Rappeller and in two minutes, get to the other side." Alex held out the stopwatch hanging around her neck. "Who's first?"

Linden stepped up to the edge of the cliff. "Me!"

Alex started her stopwatch. "Go!"

Linden attached the rope behind him, threw his Rappeller across the plunging ravine, and watched as it sucked onto the opposite cliff face. With a determined expression he grabbed onto the rope and climbed above the boiling rapids with the ease of someone crossing a street. When he reached the other side, he pressed the release button and stood proudly on the opposite cliff.

Alex pressed her stopwatch.

"One minute twenty. Well done. Max?"

Max stepped up to the cliff edge. The swirling waters below made her feel dizzy. Her head felt like it was melting and her breath came in short, sharp jabs.

"Go!"

Max tried to make her feet move, but with every second that passed they seemed to become heavier, like they were made of cement. No matter how hard she tried, her fear of heights wouldn't let her budge.

"Max?"

"I . . . I . . ." she began, but felt like she'd forgotten how to speak. She wanted so badly to do it, but couldn't. Her eyes blurred so that the cliff and the abyss merged into one giant fog. Why couldn't she move?

"Time's up," said Alex, and left the room in a stinging silence.

When Max and Linden met her in the main training

area, she was making notes on her computer. It seemed like ages until she spoke.

"Linden. You did well. You have a natural ability." Silence again, before, "And Max?"

Her heart perked up. "Yes?"

"Sometimes you have to look fear in the face to realize it's not so terrifying."

Max's shoulders nosedived along with her ego. She knew she wasn't perfect, but she was a good spy and she'd get it soon. She realized it was probably the wrong moment, but she asked anyway. "Alex? When will we be sent on our next mission?"

Alex started packing her bag. "That is unclear, but it certainly won't be until you have mastered a lot more. I'll see you both tomorrow. On time."

As Max watched her go, she was determined to prove to her she was a good spy.

Her body ached and her pride sagged, but that wasn't the worst of it. She had a science exam tomorrow and faced hours of study when all she felt like was falling into a deep, training-free sleep.

**CHAPTER 6**

Terror at
Hollingdale

*Brrrt! Brrrt! Brrrt! Brrrt!*

Max's head shot up. Her clock shouted the digital numbers: 7:00. She'd slept the whole night slumped over her science books. Great! She couldn't even remember what she'd studied before she fell asleep.

When Max's mother drove them to school, Max tried to make a quick getaway before her mother did anything to embarrass her. But it was like she couldn't help herself as she called out, "Sweetie, do you have your lunch?"

Max could see the other kids mimicking her mother and calling her "sweetie." She nodded and moved away fast.

"This school's huge," Linden gasped. "I'd like to meet some of the other kids."

"There aren't any worth meeting." Max was still being called "sweetie" from somewhere behind her. "And make sure you don't do anything to draw attention to yourself."

But just as she said it, Max slammed into Mrs. Flagbottom, the sports teacher, and her bulging crate of balls. Max fell to the ground, a frenzied whirl of rubber bouncing around her. The usual laughter followed from everyone within a ten-mile radius, but the laughter that hurt most was from Linden.

Max's look soon told him to stop. "Oh come on, Max, it is funny," he tried, but she wouldn't hear it.

"I hate being such a klutz, especially in front of Toby."

Linden looked at where Max's eyes had landed.

"Why do you care what he thinks?"

"I don't," Max snapped. "I care that I scraped my knee when I fell and no one seems worried about that."

Linden looked at Toby. He couldn't see why Max would worry about what he thought, but then there were lots of things about Max that Linden couldn't work out.

"Okay, settle down, class." Mrs. Grimshore knew the extra talking was due to exam nerves. "Before we start, I'd like to introduce you to Linden. He's our guest at Hollingdale this week—a friend of Max's from a school in Pennsylvania. He's here on our exchange program."

Max shrunk as someone nearby clucked like a chicken.

"I know you'll do your best to make him feel welcome." Mrs. Grimshore frowned. "Linden will go on with his own work while the rest of us have the pleasure of this exam."

The class groaned as she handed out the test.

Toby leaned into Linden and pointed to the side of the classroom. "That's a computer. We've got a lot of those in the city."

"Mrs. Grimshore?" It was Linden. Toby shot him a threatening glare. "Can I do the exam too?"

"I don't see why not, especially as I've never had anyone volunteer for an exam before."

Linden let out one of his super smiles. Toby thought maybe he wasn't a pushover after all.

Max yawned and slumped across her desk.

"You may begin."

When Max turned hers over, terror rose inside her like an electric charge and her stomach lurched, threatening to bring up her breakfast. She'd studied all the wrong things. She looked around. All the other kids seemed to be flying through. Especially Toby.

The next thirty minutes were the longest of her life and when the recess bell rang, she didn't know if she should be relieved or run away and join the circus.

She sat under a tree with Linden eating a giant sandwich.

"Oh no," Max moaned. "Here comes Toby."

"Who's your new friend, Max?"

She didn't answer. Hadn't the morning been bad enough?

Linden stood up. "Linden Franklin." He munched his sandwich.

Toby was shocked. Usually kids were more scared of him.

"Not too hard for you, our city exam? Guess none of it made sense coming from the country."

"It was easy. We did plant structures and food chains last year. I guess we must be ahead of you. Anyhow, I didn't take it for credit."

Toby knew Max was enjoying every minute of this, but he wasn't finished yet.

"So you have spy adventures with Max?"

Max freaked. She hadn't told Linden that a few weeks before Toby had stolen her spy notebook and not only that, had read it aloud in front of the whole class.

"They're just stories, lamebrain," Max said. "As if we'd really be spies."

"Yeah." Linden beamed at Max. "We couldn't be spies, we're just kids." They collapsed into a squall of laughter as the school bell rang and Toby was left wondering what was so funny.

On the way to class, Max's palm computer vibrated in her bag with a message. She and Linden ducked behind a tree.

"Ben? How are you calling us?" she asked.

"We've got palm computers too."

"Since when?"

"Years now. Sorry to call you at school, but we'll pick you up after training. We've got great news to tell you."

"Is it about the Time and Space Machine?" Linden asked.

"We'll tell you everything tonight."

Ben zapped off the screen as Max suddenly forgot all about her exam. "I bet it's finished!"

Max looked up and saw the last of the kids pile into class and knew they couldn't afford to look suspicious. "We better go."

She put the palm computer in her pocket as they

stepped out from behind the tree. Toby watched them from across the yard. He knew they were up to something but he hadn't seen clearly enough to know what.

"You're up to something, Remy. I know it and I'm going to watch you real closely to find out what."

**CHAPTER 7**

# An Evil
# Interception

Max's next training session only confirmed she had the most clumsy, malfunctioning body that was ever built, and judging from Alex's silence, she thought the same thing too. After spending the night falling, tripping, and tumbling, Max fell to the floor from the vibrating horizontal ladder for what felt like the hundredth time. "Why couldn't I have been given a body that actually works?" she moaned into the foam mat.

Alex looked at her like she was a pet that couldn't be trained. "That's all for this evening."

Max stood up, her arm sore from banging against the wall of the Simulated Earthquake Chamber. "Bye, Alex."

She kept her eyes on her computer and muttered, "Bye."

Max turned, dragging her bag behind her like it was made of lead.

"Well, how did it go?" Ben asked when they got in the car.

"Good," said Linden, trying not to be too enthusiastic. He was still being brilliant at everything Alex asked him to do.

Ben read Max's silence. "Tough, eh? Don't worry. It gets easier."

*It better*, thought Max. *Or someone's going to have to scoop me up with a shovel after the next session.* Then she remembered. "What's your great news?"

"We'll tell you when we get to the Spy Force lab." Francis grinned cockily.

After the usual shower cap, white suit, cleansing, and temperature check procedures at the lab, Max, Linden, Ben, and Francis stood in front of the new and improved Time and Space Machine.

"American scientists have been studying the technology needed to create a Time and Space Machine for years. With everything that Einstein said, we knew it was possible except for a few barriers we had to break through and now, thanks to a precious stone from a small Scottish town, we've done it. I'd like to introduce you to the Transporter Mark II."

Max's heart flipped in her chest and she took a deep breath to get it back into rhythm.

"It's similar to Ben's Matter Transporter, but with a little more style. Much like designing the first Model T Ford and ending up in a Ferrari." Francis smiled at Ben.

"So fashion was never a talent of mine." Ben shrugged.

Linden brushed down his suit. "We can't all be that lucky. Is this shower cap mucking up my hair?"

Ben scowled and pulled Linden's cap down over his face.

Francis continued. "Many elements have been refined and, of course, it not only transports objects but people as well."

"You did it!" Max yelled.

"You guys are brilliant!" cried Linden.

Francis blushed and focused on the Transporter Mark II.

He never liked it when people made a fuss over him.

"Let me explain how it works. As you can see, it is still a small device with a sensor/camera, power light, a rod at the side, and an LED screen with a grid. The solar cells and cord have been replaced by the energy of the Aurora Stone and the key panel has been replaced by a voice recognition system, or if you need to be quiet, by writing your request with the rod on the LED screen."

"So I can just talk to it or write down what I want?" Max asked.

"Yes. It's incredibly efficient technology. When you need to find a location, you simply tell it where you want to go and it will find the coordinates. For multiple transportation, you can still use the scanner and outline the objects or people you wish to transport or simply say where you want to go and the Transporter will transfer you and anyone holding your hand. Excellent for quick getaways. And finally, when transportation takes place, there is no loud noise, just a green flash of light and a quiet *ffffttt*."

"Can it travel through time as well?" Linden already saw himself in ancient Egypt or sailing on the *Bounty*.

"We need to do a few more checks before we try that, but we believe so."

"And remember," Ben added seriously. "This has all happened because of you, but as important as you are, it's time you were home in bed."

Max couldn't imagine ever being tired enough to sleep

again. They were standing next to the creators of one of the most important inventions in the world and they were part of making it happen.

As they left the lab, a figure sat before a radio transmitter in a very different part of the world. He was dressed in slippers and a dressing gown and sat at a large desk before an open fire. He had heard everything.

"Ben and Francis have brought me a little closer to becoming the most powerful man in the world and they don't even know it. They may think they outsmarted me last time, but they haven't even begun to know who they are dealing with," his words echoed against the steel walls circling his office, six time zones away.

**CHAPTER 8**

# The Rules for Fighting Crime

Max stood outside the training center and stared at the doors.

Linden could feel she was tense and tried to lighten her mood.

"They're not going to come to you, you know."

"I know," Max answered. "You may have noticed I haven't done very well in there over the last few days."

Linden was quiet, fearful that speaking might be dangerous for his health.

"I'm going to change all that," Max said decisively.

Linden waited. Alex hated them being late.

"Is it going to take long?"

Max shot him a glare that made him feel he was standing in front of a firing squad.

"I mean, you take all the time you need."

After a few minutes Max was ready. "Let's go," she said and strode through the doors like James Bond accepting a mission. This training session was going to be unlike any other, she'd told herself as she marched inside. Gone were the days of being a klutz. She was going to be the best, most agile agent there ever was.

"We're ready," she announced to Alex. "Where do we begin?"

Alex launched into the evening's schedule, but despite Max's resolve, this training session turned out to be worse than all the others.

The last task was to outwit the Intruder Robot, but after the tenth attempt, Max ended up scrunched in its arms, squirming like a piece of live bait.

"Okay, Max. That'll do." Alex hit the remote and the robot dropped her to the floor.

"Oooph!" Max looked up at the robot. "Maybe you could be a bit gentler next time, you hunk of technology?"

Max picked herself up while Alex finished her notes and packed her bag without a word.

"I guess that means we can go," whispered Linden.

When they were outside, Max stopped. "I forgot something," she said as she turned back toward the doors.

Linden sensed this could mean trouble. "Max?"

"Hmmm?" she mumbled innocently.

"Try not to upset her."

"Who said anything about upsetting her?"

Linden sighed as she turned on her heels and went inside. "Just a hunch."

Max stopped abruptly in front of Alex.

"Yes?"

She took a deep breath. "I think you're being really unfair and way too hard on me considering this is my first week of training, and anyone can see I'm trying as hard as I can to do everything you want me to, but for some reason you don't want to see that."

Alex studied Max as though she were a bug under a magnifying glass. Max's heart thumped and her throat seized up. Maybe she'd gone too far. Maybe Alex would refuse to train them. Maybe her big mouth had really blown it this time.

Alex said in a voice so quiet Max had to lean in to hear it, "If you want an easy ride here, then you should quit now. Spy Force isn't a holiday resort, it's an intelligence agency for fighting crime."

She said it like she was speaking to a small child, and if there was one thing Max hated, it was being spoken to like a kid. She gritted her teeth and felt her anger grow inside her, splitting imaginary clothes like the Incredible Hulk in a bad mood.

What Max wanted to say was this: "I can do anything you or Spy Force ask me to do, but what I'm really sick of is your big-headed attitude that makes me feel like I'm the biggest failure who ever lived and who will never be able to do even the simplest spy work when, in case you've forgotten, I've saved the world twice."

Max felt good until she realized she'd only said it in her head and Alex was still looking at her expectantly. "Is there something else you'd like to say, Max?"

She struggled to make her lips move, suddenly not feeling as brave as she had.

"You'll never get anywhere in this world without finding things a little hard sometimes."

Max tried to think of something to say, but came up with zero.

"Now, have a good night's sleep and I'll see you tomorrow."

There was nothing else for Max to do but walk outside to where Linden was waiting.

"Are we in for it? Because I don't think my body can take any more perfecting," Linden joked, flexing his muscles.

Max didn't answer.

"It's okay, Max. You'll get it."

"I know I will. I just wish she wasn't so mean." She was only just holding back a sloosh of tears.

"I guess being gushy isn't her style."

Max looked up and smiled, but as she did, she saw someone across the street staring straight at her.

"Hey, I think I've seen that guy before."

"Which guy?"

A bus pulled up on the opposite side of the street and when it drove off, the man was gone.

"He was there. At the bus stop."

"Maybe he wanted to catch the bus." Linden tried to say it without sounding sarcastic but decided he hadn't done a very good job. "You've had a rough day. Maybe you shouldn't trust your eyes tonight."

Max sighed. "You're right."

"I know." Linden smiled. "You better get used to that. It happens a lot."

"You kids going to stand there all night or do you want a lift?" It was Ben.

Every bit of Max's body and pride was bruised and sore, and as she got in the car, there was only one place she wanted to be. "Hi, Ben. Can you take us home, please?"

CHAPTER 9

A Dark and
Terrible Secret

"It says here in the event of high pursuit on snow, the Silver Snowbeast is the only way to escape. It is a twin-engine high-speed buggy that is compact, made completely of natural materials and has a built-in parachute for quick aerial getaways."

"Really?" Max leaned her chin on her hand and focused all her energy on trying to lift her head.

Linden sensed Max wasn't listening.

"And then there's the Minotaur, a single-seater glider that moves through the air in complete silence and runs on the wind of elephant farts."

"That's great," Max murmured.

"Max, did you stay up all night again?"

"I've got to prove to Alex I can be a good spy."

"I think even spies go to sleep sometimes."

"Max! We're late, sweetie. Are you and your friend ready?"

*If she doesn't use Linden's name soon, I'm leaving home,* Max thought as she dragged herself off her bed and downstairs.

When they arrived at school, Toby was the first person they saw. Suddenly Max's feeling of being a total failure reached new heights.

"Hey, Max? Ready for your exam results?" Toby pasted on one of those grins toothpaste companies love.

Max tried to ignore him. Why do some people seem to have everything? He's good-looking, popular, has good grades, and always gets everything right.

Max stepped into class and yawned as she found her desk. Mrs. Grimshore started talking and Max tried to concentrate. But then something very strange happened.

"Now, class, I've come across some exceptional students in my seventy-five years of teaching, but I've rarely come across one so gifted." Mrs. Grimshore was in a much better mood than usual and, Max noticed only now, had a bright blue hairdo and giant teeth.

"I would like to award the prize of Student of the Year to Max Remy."

The whole class cheered. Max looked up. Was it true? Could she have finally beaten Toby? And she thought she hadn't even passed! As she walked to the front of the class, she saw Toby in tears. Kids from all around called her name. "Max! Max! Max!"

She'd done it!

"Max! Max! Max!"

"Max!"

Max sucked in a gulp of air and wiped a line of dribble from her mouth.

"I'm not exciting enough for you this morning?" It was Mrs. Grimshore, with her normal teeth and hair. *Please don't let it be a dream,* thought Max.

"And this is for you." Max saw the fat D on the exam paper and knew it was real as was Toby's whale-size grin.

"Congratulations, Toby. First place." There was polite

applause from the class. "But we have an equal first place. Linden Franklin."

Linden blushed. He liked science but hated when people made a big deal of when he did well.

At the end of class, as if Max's life wasn't miserable enough, Toby and his friends made an appearance.

"What happened, Max? Leave your brain home on the day of the exam?"

Max wished the Time and Space Machine was with her now so she could program herself right out of there.

"Maybe you were just too busy to study." He winked at his friends. "Or maybe you were spending too much time with your boyfriend."

Max fired up a deep red. After what she'd been through in the last few days, she'd had enough. She flung her hands on her hips and got ready to let him have it. "Listen, Jennings. You think you're so smart, but there are some kids who have done things much cleverer than you could even think of."

"Like what?" Toby savored his next jibe. "Be a super-spy?"

Linden knew Max was being baited and in the state she was in, if Toby pushed hard enough, she just might reveal their involvement in Spy Force.

"For your information—"

An announcement cackled across the schoolyard, stopping Max from saying anything else.

Linden quickly got them away from Toby. "Where's our next class?" he asked as he led Max away.

"Why does he have to be such a jerk? Where does it say his name is Toby Jennings and he'll be a massive pain in the—"

"He does seem to have developed a knack for it."

"Knack for it? He wrote the manual on jerkdom. He's a fat-headed, conceited, arrogant nobody *and* he called you my *boyfriend*!"

Linden looked offended. "And here I was thinking I was a good catch."

Max felt herself calm down. "Now that one definitely came from your mom."

Linden pouted. "You don't think it's true?"

She laughed. "Let's just say she might have been a bit biased."

"Max? Can I say something that might make you mad?"

"Depends on how long you want to live," she said warily.

"I think Toby picks on you because he likes you."

Max had seen and heard some amazing things in the last few months. She'd flown across the world in seconds using the Time and Space Machine, been sucked into the heart of Spy Force via the Wall of Goodness, and been a passenger on the hyperfast Invisible Jet, but this was the most crazy.

"Toby like me? Are you nuts? Toby can't stand me.

Toby's aim is to make my life a misery. Toby's the most popular guy in school. How could Toby even possibly like me?"

"Just a thought." But Linden wasn't convinced, and by the amount of times Max said Toby's name, he wasn't sure she was either.

The rest of Max's day blurred around her. Teachers. Classes. Students. She was worried about training and the Spy Force exam. She'd made a mess of everything so far and she really needed to do well to prove to Alex she was a good spy.

At the end of the day, Max saw her mother waving and calling from across the street. "Sweetie," she yelled in front of everyone. "Quickly. We're in a hurry."

"Do you think she deliberately tries to embarrass me?"

"From what I've seen, I think it comes naturally." Linden shrugged.

"Great. So it's for life." She sighed. "Better go. Training's going to be fun compared to what Mom's going to do to me when she hears about that exam."

Despite what Max expected, training wasn't so bad after all. Like things suddenly clicked and her body started to cooperate. She successfully maneuvered her way through the Infrared Night Vision Enemy Hideout course and managed to infiltrate a maximum security Bad Guy Lair to save a captured Spy Force agent. At the end of the session, she was exhausted and stood before Alex hoping she'd be happy too.

Alex looked up. "That's all for today."

That was it? After finally being good at something, that's all she had to say? Max was starting to get sick of how hard it was for Alex to say anything nice.

She and Linden turned and started to walk out, when Alex stopped them.

"Max? Can I see you for a minute?"

*See me? What for?* Max had that awful being-sent-to-the-principal feeling.

Linden gave her a warm smile. "I'll wait outside."

"Sit down," Alex said.

Max sat, not knowing what was going to happen. *Please don't tell me I'm not spy material,* she pleaded silently. *Please don't tell me that.*

"I know you think I'm being hard on you, Max, but the best lesson I've learned in life is that you have to look after yourself. Once you know that, no matter what situation you get caught in, no matter how frightening, you'll be able to give it your best shot to get out of it."

"That's not true!"

Alex's head tilted in annoyance and Max thought maybe she'd been too harsh.

"Well, not all of it anyway." Max felt scared, but now that she'd started, she had to keep going. "It's good to be able to save yourself but there's nothing wrong with relying on other people as well."

Alex's expression softened like she was trying to work out how to say the next part.

"Can I tell you something you can never tell anyone?"

Max felt her body stiffen. She'd wanted so badly to be friends with Alex, but now that she was about to tell her something secret, all she wanted to do was run.

"I'm not sure what you know about me, but I was the youngest person ever to be inducted into Spy Force."

Max perked up. "I know. You were nine years old and always wanted to be a spy since reading about them when you were little and because your dad was in Spy Force too."

"He was the bravest man ever, but during a dangerous mission we were on, he died."

Alex's lips sandwiched tightly together. This must have been the mission that had been deleted from *The Guide to Spy Force Missions.*

"There was another spy on the mission with us. He was my dad's best friend. I'd known him all my life and called him Uncle Larry. I was fifteen. We were in the building of an enemy agent that had been blown up and was collapsing around us. Walls and ceilings were crashing down and the floor was crumbling like chalk dust under our feet." Alex's words were like an ice storm, sticking Max to the spot.

"I was following Uncle Larry and my dad was following me, making sure I was okay. We were running along a corridor dodging falling debris when I heard this crash behind me. The floor between Dad and me had collapsed into a dusty pit, leaving Dad trapped beneath a tangle of beams. I turned to Uncle Larry for what we should do next as another piece of roof crashed behind us. Uncle Larry looked me in the eye and said, 'We'll have to leave him.' I wasn't going anywhere without my dad, but then Dad spoke up and told us to get out before we were killed."

Alex took a quick gasp of air.

"I only saw him for five seconds after that, before the floor beneath him gave way and he was gone."

Without another word, Alex picked up her bag and walked away.

Linden stuck his head round the door and saw Max alone on the bench. The way her shoulders drooped, he knew things hadn't gone well.

He sat down beside her. "Max, sometimes things don't go the way we want them to for a reason, even if we can't see it at the time. That was one of Mom's best sayings."

Linden could see she didn't want to talk. "Come on, let's go."

At home, Max's mother was waiting at the door. "Max, Linden. Come in."

Something was wrong. Max could feel it. Max's mother had this gigantic smile and sounded so sweet it felt like a dental hazard just standing near her.

And another thing. She'd actually said Linden's name.

"Mrs. Grimshore called."

*Of course,* Max thought. *She knows about the exam.*

"She was shocked by your performance and asked if

everything was okay at home. Of course, I said it was and suggested that perhaps your friend's visit was too distracting and wouldn't happen again if things didn't improve."

"Okay," said Max in a wilting tone.

Linden was surprised. He knew Max hated being spoken to like that and that her exam had nothing to do with his stay. Usually she would have defended herself, but all she could think about as she climbed the stairs to her room was Alex and her dad. Everything else seemed a long way away.

CHAPTER 10

An Important
Job and a Pair of
Evil Hands

**Chronicles of Spy Force:**

Alex Crane and Max Remy ran through the tangle of collapsed columns, roof beams, and broken glass and jumped aside just in time to avoid a barrel-size potted plant that rolled their way.

"Are you two okay?" Agent Crane called from behind.

"Yeah, Dad. You?"

"Yeah." He gave one of his famous lopsided smiles to his daughter and her friend. He was proud of both of them as they ran through the collapsing building without a shred of fear.

The building was an old warehouse on the Hudson River in New York, and Max, Alex, and her dad had infiltrated it to stop the forgery of great artworks that Spy Force had traced there. But a deadly tip-off by an arch enemy now saw the building collapsing around them.

Without warning, a loud crash punctured the rumbling din. Alex and Max were pushed forward by the blast and fell to the ground. When they looked behind, they saw a giant slab of floor had collapsed and Alex's father with it.

"Dad!" Alex screamed as she saw him pinned under great weights of steel and concrete.

Max and Alex pushed the blanket of rubble off them as they crawled over the crumbling pile of debris toward him.

"Stop. It's too dangerous," Alex's father called.

"We're not leaving you," Max shouted, but the floor's

crumbling hold began to give way. They had to save him. He was one of Spy Force's best agents. And he was Alex's dad. If they could only reach out a little further. Just a little . . .

Max was finishing her entry when the vibrations of her palm computer interrupted. She looked at the blinking device and knew she'd better answer it.

"Ah, Max, you must have been up early," Steinberger said cheerily. "I was worried I might find you in your pajamas. You seem to be a late starter."

Max looked at her clothes. She'd fallen asleep studying again.

"Yeah. It feels like I never went to bed."

"I wanted to wish you luck for your exam. I'll be supervising. It's normally Dretch, but he's been called away."

"That's a shame," said Max, a creeping chill covering her at the mention of that name. "Has Alex told you how we've been doing?"

"Not yet. She likes to give a full report at the end."

"Oh." Max was hoping she'd said something.

"I'll see you both in an hour." Steinberger zapped off her screen.

"Max, are you decent?" It was Linden.

"Are you?"

"I try to be."

"Come in then."

Linden was as perky as ever. "Ready for the exam?"

"Is a Microsubsonic Atomizer a great way to drive bad guys' ears crazy underwater?"

"Was Anna Purday the first agent to cross the Himalayas using only the Polar Sustenance Shield?" Linden added.

"Was 1972 the first year Spy Force won the Agency of the Year Award?"

Linden smiled. "Been studying, eh? It's a long exam. What about your mom?"

"She's shopping, which means she'll be out all day."

When Steinberger reappeared, Max and Linden were ready for him.

"Each of you will sit on opposite sides of Max's desk. The exam will appear on your palm computers with me sitting in the corner of your screens to supervise. Don't let that put you off. I'll be very quiet. You have three hours and your time . . . starts . . . now."

Linden shot a quick wink at Max for luck and they began.

Max looked at the first question and was relieved when she saw she knew it. Her fingers scurried across the keys like frantic ants, eating up every question and racing to the next. When the final moments elapsed, the exam disappeared and Steinberger's face filled the screen again. "Time's up."

Max and Linden flopped back in their chairs.

"On behalf of Spy Force, I'd like to thank you both for all your hard work this week. Spy work can be very difficult, especially while trying to keep up your regular life without anyone knowing about your other life. Even the best spies find that hard. And now," he said with an enlivened pause, "we have a job for you."

"A mission?" Max perked up. After all this time they were finally going on another mission.

"Kind of." Steinberger looked uneasy. "Quite a few agents here have been struck down with a very bad flu. Pesky thing. We can walk on the moon but we can't control some sniffles and a stuffed-up head. Anyhow, we need your help."

Linden's head filled with images of glaciers in New Zealand, deserts in Algeria, reefs off Australia. "Anything, Steinberger. Just name it."

"We'd like you to be waiters at the Annual Spy Awards Night."

Waiters? Not only had Max not been invited but she was asked to be a waiter. She wanted to be a guest.

It wasn't quite what Linden had expected, but he thought it could be fun. "Sure."

"Excellent." As Steinberger told them what their duties would be, Max scowled. *I'll never see any action as a waiter. All I'll see is soup and trays and the backs of people's heads as they tuck into a life that is exciting and adventurous and has nothing to do with me.*

"I've told Ben and Francis and they have agreed to let you use the Time and Space Machine as Sleek also has the flu and his sinuses really act up when he travels long distances in the Invisible Jet. Your mother has been told they'll pick you up tomorrow morning at seven and you'll be home late. That will give you plenty of time to finish your duties once the awards are over."

*Why is there always something wrong with my life?* Max thought. *When school is good, there's always Toby. When home is good, there's Aidan, and now that I'm about to go on a great adventure, there's a big pile of dirty dishes.*

"That's all for now. I'll see you tomorrow when you arrive at Spy Force," Steinberger finished cheerfully.

Linden looked at a deflated Max. "It could be worse."

"How?"

"We could have been asked to clean the toilets."

"Errrr." Max threw her pillow at Linden.

"Just trying to be helpful."

As Max and Linden talked about the exam, a gloved hand outside Max's house clutched a radio transmitter and a man spoke into his jacket lapel. "Radio transmission complete. What would you like me to do now, boss?"

A voice whined from the other side of the world.

"We've just been delivered a little bonus," came the reply. "Not only will we be the new owners of a brand-new Time and Space Machine but we almost have all we need to finally undo Harrison and Spy Force."

**CHAPTER 11**

A Mission Begins

Max and Linden were packed and ready when Ben and Francis picked them up the next day. Ben was acting a little strange, double-checking everything and saying things twice. "I don't mind telling you I'm a little jealous. Using the Time and Space Machine *and* being invited to the Spy Awards Night. It's a very special invitation. It's an honor. A real honor."

"We've been invited to be waiters," Max reminded him as they drove ever closer to the lab.

"We know. We know. It's a very important job. Very important. Serving some of the greatest unsung heroes of our day. Saving the world while most of us have no idea we're even in danger."

When it was put that way, Max felt better about what they were about to do. Maybe it wasn't going to be such a bad job after all.

Max watched as the lab appeared before them, and after being waved through by the security guards, Max, Ben, Francis, and Linden went through the necessary procedures for getting ready for the lab, including wearing their white suits.

When they finally stood in front of the Transporter Mark II, a tremor shot through Max's body. "Do you remember the first time we used the old Time and Space Machine?" she asked Linden.

"Yeah." He looked down at his bulging white lab suit

that Ben had given him to wear. "I was dressed a little better, but this should be fun too."

Max smiled. Apart from his corny jokes, Linden would always be first choice as her spy partner.

"Do you remember how the Transporter works?" Francis asked.

"Yep," Linden and Max said together, eager to get on with it. After the last week of training and studying, they felt ready for anything.

"Be careful out there, very careful," Ben said somberly. "It can be a dangerous business."

"Handing out soup?" Linden asked.

"Well, not the soup bit . . . all the other stuff."

"We'll be fine." Max was worried Ben was going to get all emotional as he leaned down and wrapped her in one of his hugs.

"You're very special to us. Both of you. Very special. You know that?"

"Yeah, I know," Max wheezed.

After Linden had his dose of Ben's hugging, they were ready to go, when Max's pocket vibrated. She opened her palm computer.

"Aunt Eleanor?" Max was surprised to see her aunt.

"Max. Thank goodness I caught you."

"Are you using Ben's palm computer?"

"I have my own. We've had them for years. The first

ones were really huge, but they're much more streamlined now."

"Why didn't you tell me you all had one?"

"You know we can't tell you things before Spy Force lets us," Eleanor said gently.

"What else don't I know? Next you'll be telling me you have a deep underground cavern in the farm that doubles as a secret high-tech laboratory."

Max thought she saw Ben and Francis exchange a quick glance.

"Aunt Eleanor?"

"Ah . . . I should let you go. The Spy Awards nights are very special events. I'm sure you'll be great."

Just as she spoke, they heard an enormous crash in the background.

"What was that?"

"It's Larry," Eleanor explained. "He's climbed onto the roof again."

"There's going to be hail," Eleanor said. Linden and Ben nodded.

Eleanor and Ben were the only people Max knew who had a weather-predicting pig. Despite knowing she was going to regret asking, there was a part of her that had to know.

"Why does Larry climb on the roof when it's going to hail?"

"He likes to pretend he's a giant piece of ice plummeting to earth. Anyway, dear, better let you go. Best of luck and may the Force be with you."

"Larry's on the roof." Linden was disappointed.

"Yeah." Ben sounded the same. "He makes this big pile out of hay and old rags and then he dives into it. Doesn't hail much, so we don't see it often, but it's great when it happens."

"Do you remember the time when a gust of wind blew up and he got stuck on the clothesline?" Linden sniggered.

"It took all three of us an hour to get him down, but then he went straight back up on the roof again."

"He's a brave one, that pig." Linden smiled affectionately.

Max watched Ben and Linden as they mused about Larry's pig-flying abilities.

"Is it too much to ask to actually get on with our mission?"

"Oh, yeah." Ben shook his head. "Francis?"

"Let's all hold hands."

*Hold hands?* Max thought. *It's a spy mission, not a hippie convention.*

"Today is a very big day in the history of the scientific world and the advancement of mankind . . . I mean, humankind. Max and Linden," Francis continued, "we wish you luck as you embark on a great journey. It's not by sitting still that people become great. It's by taking risks and moving ahead. May the Force be with you."

Ben struggled with a tear tickling the corner of his eye as Max released her hand. "We better go."

"Call us on your palm computers when you get there," Ben's voice cracked as Max tried to get out of there before she had to witness an adult cry.

"Okay." She wrote *Spy Force* on the LED screen of the Transporter Mark II and it immediately displayed the coordinates.

"This is much quicker than before," Linden exclaimed.

"And take care," Ben added in a voice slightly higher than normal. "Lots of care."

"Sure."

"And don't forget to . . ."

But it was too late. Max grabbed Linden's hand, said "Transport," and just as Francis had told them, there was no loud noise, only a green flash of light, a quiet *fffftttt,* and they were gone.

**CHAPTER 12**

# VART Landing and Kitty Litter Poop

A flash of fluorescent light billowed from the air, and tiny sparks of color fell like a shower from a fireworks display. Max and Linden appeared from the center of the light and hung suspended in the air for a few seconds before floating gently to the ground.

Watching from nearby, Steinberger pressed down on his stopwatch.

"Fifteen seconds! Brilliant!" he whispered to himself. "Not quite the speed we'd like yet, but they've done it. Ben and Francis have to be two of the most ingenious people to ever get up in the morning."

Dressed in their white lab suits, Max and Linden arrived at Spy Force in the Vehicular All-Response Tower, or the VART for short. Linden landed on his feet looking pretty similar to how he left. Max, however, looked like a giant upside-down ice cream sundae, as her suit had filled with air during transportation and she'd landed on a pile of kitty litter and some freshly laid poop.

"What is it with animals relieving themselves right where I'm about to land? The world's not that small," Max said as she stretched her head over her expanded body to see the Transporter Mark II safely nestled in her hand. "*And* cats have to have the smelliest poop in the world."

Dretch's cat, Delilah, chose that moment to saunter in front of Max looking like a proud goose that had laid a golden egg. "You may think you've won this one, but just you wait," Max warned.

Linden stared at his upturned friend. "Max, she's a cat. She doesn't speak English."

"'She knows what I'm saying," Max sneered as the cat innocently licked its fur.

"Ah, Max! Linden!" Steinberger walked toward them with a sprightly step, then suddenly stopped. "What is that smell?"

"It's Delilah's welcome-home present for Max," Linden explained. "I'm trying not to take it personally that I didn't get anything."

"And who's become a little chubby since I last saw her?" Steinberger poked Max's overinflated suit and giggled.

At that exact moment Linden thought Steinberger was just about the bravest person he knew.

Max didn't smile and Steinberger's expression collapsed into a frown.

"Maybe you should just help me up?"

Steinberger pulled a small sewing kit from his pocket. "Another thing Nana said never to be without, along with a hanky." He produced a shiny needle and plunged it into Max's suit so that she flew through the air like an escaped party balloon.

"Waaaaaaa!" she yelled as she fizzled in front of Linden and Steinberger.

"This is better than a fair," said Linden, knowing there was no way Max would hear him.

"Maybe she should be part of the finale for tonight's celebrations?" Steinberger was buoyed by his own humor until Max, who was no longer airborne, came crashing to the floor with a loud, "Oooooph!"

Linden and Steinberger leaped into action.

"Max, are you all right?" Steinberger asked anxiously.

Max groaned as she tried to sit up. "Now I know how the scarecrow in the *The Wizard of Oz* felt."

Linden and Steinberger looked at each other. Max realised she'd told a joke, which felt very unMaxlike. Linden opened his mouth to speak.

"Don't say anything," said Max. "I'm just as confused as you are. Let's go."

Max put the Transporter Mark II in her pack while Linden called Ben and Francis to tell them they'd arrived safely. She looked around the VART at the Sleek Machine, the Space Explorer, and the area where the Invisible Jet would be if she could see it. As much as she was angry about her landing, she was happy to be back at Spy Force.

Stepping onto the Vibratron 5000 for identification, they felt the familiar tingling sensation throughout their bodies. "I love this part," Linden said when it was his turn.

"Are we going to Harrison's office now?" Max secretly hoped Harrison might have a mission for them and besides, she was sure he'd want to say hello to his top spies.

"I'm afraid not. Harrison is busy with the heads of all

the other agencies, going over final security details for this evening. Meanwhile, let's get you fitted out."

Steinberger led the way down a series of long, dimly lit corridors until they reached the kitchen and the bright blue-and-red-striped hairdo of Irene.

"Thank goodness you're here. Quick, try this."

She held out a tray of hot pink muffins smothered in an orange-colored sauce.

Linden didn't need to be asked twice. "Mmmmm."

"Is that a good *mmm* or a bad one?" Irene looked nervous.

"Can you come and live at my place?"

Irene's face stretched into a wide grin. "They're going on the menu."

Linden liked Irene, especially the way she reminded him of his mother. They both had rounded figures, wore bright colors, and always had a positive word for even the bleakest situation.

"I'm in charge of the kitchen tonight and you and I will be working together."

"All right!" Suddenly Linden didn't care if he wasn't on a mission. He was going to spend the night surrounded by slightly weird but delicious food.

Steinberger held out two coat hangers with long, dark plastic covers.

"These are your outfits for tonight and your security passes, which you must keep on you at all times."

Max grabbed her uniform knowing the chances of it

looking any good were close to zero, but at least she could get rid of her kitty-littered lab suit.

After Steinberger showed them to some changing rooms, Max stomped out wearing black trousers, a white shirt and a black vest. All way too big. Linden's uniform was the same except, of course, it was a perfect fit.

"Is it too much to ask that I wear something that fits while trying to save the world?" Max asked.

"Sorry about that," Steinberger apologized. "The other waiters were bigger than you and there was no time to get new ones."

*Beep, beep, beep, beep.* Steinberger's pager beeped.

"I have to go," he said in an urgent tone. "I'll leave you in Irene's capable hands."

"What's wrong?" Max needed to know in case there was a terrible disaster she could help out with or a calamitous incident only she could fix.

"It's my dry cleaning. My suit's ready for tonight."

Steinberger disappeared as Max stood in a pool of disappointment.

"Right." Irene slapped her floured hands together. "Let's get to work. There's a lot to do before the awards can begin."

Linden followed Irene eagerly as Max trudged behind.

"Watch out, everyone. This is where my life gets really fascinating," she mumbled as she pulled her baggy pants higher.

"We'll start with finger food," Irene continued. "Agents are an introverted lot. Cagey and quiet. Never give anything away. Part of the job. It's our task to limber them up, make them come out of themselves, and this is how we'll do it. We'll start with French toast with blue honey mashed potatoes and red fish eggs all the way from Australia, Russian squid stuffed with bright yellow zucchini flowers, and black truffles from the Black Forest in Germany, and finally, organic farm-raised frogs' legs lightly fried and dipped in wasabi and soy sauce—a little favorite of Harrison's."

"And that's going to limber them up?" Apart from the time Toby Jennings pulled out his tooth and showed it to her, blood and all, Max had never heard anything so gross in her life.

"I'd pretty much guarantee it."

Max watched as Irene and Linden bustled around shelves with piles of ingredients, sure that she could be doing something more important than playing waitress. *And* on a night where she should be taking her place among all the other top spies of the world. Had everyone forgotten she'd helped save the world? Twice? Was it too much to ask that—

A loud clanging sound thundered behind her, followed by a screeching meow.

"Come here, my little one."

Max felt as though ice water had been poured over her and knew it could only mean one thing.

Dretch.

His small, bent body was wrapped in his wrinkled maroon coat and his sneaky eyes spun around in his eye sockets like two lost ferrets. His hair was the same shaggy mop of gray spaghetti that dribbled in front of his face and across the scar that ran down the length of his cheek and past his gray stubbled chin.

"Come to be the hired help, have you? 'Bout time they figured out where your real talents lie."

"I said I'd help." Max tried not to look as scared as she was. "As a favor to Harrison."

"Even great leaders sometimes make bad choices," Dretch sniveled.

Max folded her arms and looked toward Linden and Irene, who were oblivious of Dretch's sudden appearance.

"I haven't forgotten that you tried to blacken my name last time you were here.* And if I so much as hear you put one foot wrong, I will make sure you're thrown out of the Force quicker than your miraculous Time and Space Machine can get you home."

Max knew she'd earned Dretch's anger when she'd accused him of being a double agent, but she couldn't help feeling there was something that wasn't quite right about him. She flinched as Delilah appeared with a thump on Dretch's hunched shoulders, and after a dismissive groan that reached right into Max's bones, they left.

*For more exciting details see *Mission: Spy Force Revealed.*

**CHAPTER 13**

Potatoes and
Personal Flying
Devices

**Chronicles of Spy Force:**

Alex Crane and Max Remy walked through the narrow ravine outside the ancient city of Petra, in Jordan. Petra also meant City of Rock, and as the superspies cast their eyes over the temples, outdoor theaters, and tombs chiseled out of solid stone, they knew why. This was one of the rare moments in their lives when they weren't superspies but simple travelers, taking in the marvels of the ancient world.

Max stopped to look at the carvings on the entrance to the Treasury of the Pharaohs while Alex was lured by the intricate patterns and deep rich colors of a nearby carpet stand. A small, hooded man held a rug out to her.

"Look closer," he said in a muffled voice Alex was sure she'd heard elsewhere, but before she could remember where, a large rug was thrown over her head and she was swept off her feet.

"Max!" she shouted as she was hoisted over the man's shoulder.

"Alex?" Max turned around and scanned the ancient arena, only just catching sight of a large wriggling carpet disappearing around a stone corner.

"Alex!" Max began to run as four large hands grabbed her.

"No, no, Ms. Remy. You are coming with us."

Who were these men? What did they want? And where

was Alex? Max had to escape so she could rescue her friend before anything happened to her. Before . . .

"We're not boring you, are we, Max?"

Irene was holding a rolling pin and staring at her with wide eyes through red sparkled glasses.

"No," Max lied as she was pulled from her Alex Crane adventure to find herself standing over a giant tub of potatoes.

"Good, because when you're done with those, I've got some frogs I'd like you to meet."

On top of her overlarge waiter's suit, Max was wearing an oversize apron that had been bleached so bright she almost had to wear sunglasses, and on her head perched a white hat that had all the elegance of a collapsing tent. She'd peeled her last potato and happily thrown it into the tub when a hefty-bellied man wheeled up another tub.

"If there's one thing you'll learn about spies, they love their taters."

"Do they?" Her look dared the man to say one more word. He got the message and left quietly.

Linden, meanwhile, seemed to be enjoying every minute of their excursion into kitchen hell and had glued himself to Irene's side.

"What is it with Linden?" Max asked herself. "He

always smiles, never gets angry, and no matter what he's asked, he's always eager to help out. It's not normal. Everyone gets grumpy. It's one of those rules of being human."

She threw another potato into the tub.

"I'll bet Alex never had to peel potatoes on her way to being a great spy. At least this has got to be as bad as it gets."

But just then, things got worse.

Through the rows of metal shelves holding pots, egg beaters, whisks, sifters, and graters, Max saw another collapsing tent hat bob through the swinging doors.

There was a rabble of fussing, hello-ing and laughing before Max realized the terrible truth.

It was Ella.

"Of course," she moaned to herself. "Just when I thought I was surrounded with as much bad luck as even I can stand, she has to walk into my life."

"Max!" Linden called out. "Ella's here."

"Yippee. Start the party everybody," she mumbled as they came over.

"Hi, Max! It's great to see you again."

*Of course it is,* thought Max.

"Yeah. Great."

"Ella said we need to get ready to leave for the secret location."

*Typical,* thought Max. *Ella arrives after the hard work is done and has all the important information.*

They packed the food in containers and loaded them onto trolleys as Ella and Linden began their usual stream of high-powered chat.

"How did you get here?" Linden asked.

"By the Invisible Jet. Sleek was feeling better, so he volunteered to pick me up, but I heard you got here using the Transporter Mark II."

"Yeah! Ben and Francis finished it and think they finally have the answer to time travel as well."

"Awesome!"

"Okay, kids, it's time to get you down to Quimby to get your equipment," Irene interrupted Ella and Linden and saved Max's life. If she'd had to listen one second longer to this touching reunion scene, she was going to fall into a deathly coma.

Then Max was struck by what Irene had said. "Quimby? Are we going on a mission after all?"

"Because we'll be on maximum security alert this evening, all agents have been equipped by the lab in case of an emergency. Purely precautionary I'm afraid, Max." Irene smiled gently, knowing how desperate Max was for a mission.

On the way to the lab, Linden and Ella babbled on about their spy training. Ella had done hers in London and, of course, had had a great time and was probably an expert at everything.

"There's still so much to learn," she added.

*I'll say*, thought Max. *Like knowing when you're not welcome.* But then Max saw something that made her puke-covered day even worse.

"The Wall of Goodness!" Ella cried, like Christmas had come early.

"Do we have to go through this again?" Max found it hard to hide her contempt.

"It's the only way we can get to the lab. Besides," said Irene, trying to encourage her, "it'll be fun."

"If you've had your brain rearranged and covered with Jell-O." Max scowled as they approached the wall and stood perfectly still.

The Wall of Goodness was a security procedure that allowed a person entry once it had assessed their level of goodness. As expected, after a few seconds the atoms in the impenetrable-looking stone wall began reconfiguring as it wrapped itself around the visitors in a gurgling, squelchy blob.

"I love this part," shouted Irene as she was being squished like a ball of human dough, but before she could say any more, she was sucked through to the other side in one custardy squelch.

"All right!" yelled Ella as the wall massaged her into a fit of unstoppable giggles. Slurp! Ella also disappeared.

*Of course*, Max thought, *Ms. Perfect had to go next, didn't she?*

"Aaah!" Max watched as Linden was also gobbled up by the rocky, gurgling procedure.

After a few more moments of slobbering, Max had had enough. "Listen, wall. Now, let's not get smart about this, okay? You and I went through this the last time I was here and nothing has changed since then.* You can play your massage game all day if you like, but I'm good and I've got important work to do."

The wall then did something strange. It hiccupped and spluttered, like it was running out of energy.

"Wall? What's going on?"

More spluttering and chugging and still Max wasn't let through.

"Wall, you're starting to freak me out. I told you I was good, so what's your—

Before she could finish, the wall spat her out like a bowling ball in a powerful, tumbling splat.

"Max, you're here. Now we can begin," Quimby said to a mangled Max after she slid to a stop in the center of the lab.

"There's gotta be a better way to do that," Max complained as she unwound herself and stood with the others.

Quimby's normally unruly hair was pulled up on her head in a plaited and coiled nest and her usual colorful trainers had been replaced by high-heeled shoes and shimmery stockings.

"Welcome back to Spy Force. In your packs you'll find a flashlight, a pocket knife, a laser, and the Rappeller that you've all used during training," Quimby began. "There's

*For more exciting details see *Mission: Spy Force Revealed.*

also the Silencio, which when sprayed, makes a person completely silent, and the Freeze Ray, which renders a person unable to move. Finally, the Slimer, which coats your enemies in a purple chewy slime making it hard for them to move. The slime was created in Spy Force's Plantorium and is made totally of plant-based materials. Be very careful, though. These last three devices may not work properly in extreme temperatures, and always keep their safety latches on when not in use."

Quimby picked up one of the packs. "These may look like regular packs, but if you pull this toggle, they transform into Personal Flying Devices, or PFDs. PFD also stands for Personal Flotation Device, which the pack will do if you happen to make a watery landing. The lever at the side extends from the bag and controls speed and direction. They can be a little tricky to handle, like the first time Spider-Man tried to use his webslinger, but once you get the hang of it, you won't want to come down."

They each put their packs on and pulled the toggle. A soft *whhhppp* sound was heard as a small mechanical device poked out from the bottom of their packs.

"The PFD will fly in whatever direction you push the lever. To fly up, pull the lever toward you. Push it hard to go fast and softly to go slow. The button at the end of the lever is for stopping. Press that and the PFD will slowly bring you in for landing. Off you go."

Ella and Linden extended their levers and pulled them

toward them. Slowly they lifted off the ground, and after a little fumbling they seemed to get the hang of the PFD.

"Your turn, Max," Quimby encouraged her.

Max put her hand on the lever and, fearing she'd make a complete fool of herself, slowly moved it toward her. She wobbled as the PFD lifted her off the floor, but with a few near tumbles and swaggers she moved forward and was soon flying like Linden and Ella.

Quimby watched proudly as the three young spies tackled the new device.

"This is excellent," Linden called as he flew past Max, but then she sneezed, which pushed her forward against the lever and sent her zooming across the room toward a giant balloon.

"Watch out, Max!" Ella cried.

Max tried to pull back but it was too late. She sailed into the balloon with a dull *phhhrrrrt* and slid to the floor.

Ella and Linden pressed their stop buttons and slowly landed as Quimby ran over to Max. "Are you okay?"

Max's body was fine, it was her pride that was in tatters.

"Yep," Max said as she stood up. "What is that thing?"

"A hydro balloon I am experimenting with to transport Frond's rare and delicate plants."

"Otherwise known as the thing that cushioned your fall." Linden thought it might have been funny, but now that he'd said it, he knew otherwise.

"Time to go," Quimby said. "Good luck. Hopefully

everything will be fine and you won't have to use those devices, but if you do, remember, only ever use Spy Force equipment in the line of duty."

Steinberger arrived in his new suit and, after thanking Quimby for her help, led the team to the VART.

"We've just been given word of tonight's location, which we'll reach by Invisible Jet. Sleek is feeling better and Dretch has helped prepare the jet."

*Dretch!* Max thought in horror. Maybe he'd sabotaged the jet. She still wasn't sure it wasn't him who meddled with her laser on the last mission. "Can't we go some other way?"

"Not possible, I'm afraid. Speed is of the essence."

They arrived at the VART to see Irene already there supervising loading the food, which seemed to vanish in midair.

"Very exciting, isn't it?" Steinberger said to Max, who was too busy being on Dretch-watch to notice. "It's quite a privilege to be going to an awards night. Most spies have to wait years. Why I remember when . . . ."

But before he could go on, something strange happened to him. His face turned white and he spoke in short, unintelligible spurts.

"Steinberger? What's wrong?" Max, Linden, and Ella moved closer as his breathing became difficult and beads of sweat formed so fast on his brow it looked like he was caught in his own miniature rainstorm.

"Do you remember any first aid?" Linden asked Max.

"I never wanted to do the mouth-to-mouth part, so I skipped it."

"What if you ever need it?"

"You've seen the boys in my class."

Linden thought about it. "You're right."

"Maybe he's got the flu?" Ella suggested, but when they saw who had walked into the VART, they knew it wasn't the flu.

"Sorry I'm late. Got caught with a rather mischievous piranha. Frisky things when they want to be."

Frond. Of course. The head of the Plantorium at Spy Force and the one thing that could push Steinberger so far off the cool meter, it was a wonder he ever made it back.

"Steinberger. Lovely to see you." Frond's enormous smile almost knocked him off his feet as Steinberger scrambled through his love-mushed brain for a way to say hello back.

"Er . . . how . . . aahh."

"How can anyone be so blind about someone liking them?" Linden whispered to Max as they watched the awkward performance.

"Maybe she thinks this is how he is with everyone."

"Well, she better tell us why she's here before Steinberger self-combusts."

Frond continued. "I wanted to wish you luck for tonight."

Steinberger continued to try to speak but ended up looking like a large gulping fish.

"Thanks, Frond," Linden helped out before Steinberger did himself an injury.

The jet's engine revved, signaling Sleek was ready to leave.

"Let's go, everyone. Hello, Frond," Irene called out as she walked toward them. "I love the Invisible Jet. It's the best high since the last time I went on the space shuttle."

"You were on the space shuttle?" The more time Linden spent with Irene, the more he liked her.

"Sure. Now, there's a takeoff!"

"Good-bye, everyone, and may the Force be with you." Frond waved cheerily.

They all entered the jet except for Steinberger, who almost stumbled off the platform into a barrel of plant-based fuel. Max and Linden managed to grab him just in time.

"Well caught. Even though it wouldn't have been too tragic. The fuel can also double as an excellent skin cleanser," Frond assured them.

*Can we just go?* Max thought. *Adults always have to find a way of delaying the best part of things.* But when she entered the jet, she saw Ella in her seat next to Linden.

"Thith is your captaid speakgig," interrupted Sleek's stern but slightly cloggy and flu-ridden intercom voice. "All cabid quew and passedgers prepare for takeoff. Do that

117

thig with your tray tables, and bake sure your seatbelts are firbly fastened. Take-off will be id approximately thirty secodds."

Roger, the cabin guy, abruptly told Max to find a seat while Linden and Ella talked like they'd never stop.

"Come and sit with us," Irene said gently.

Max kept her eyes on Linden and Ella and only just managed to strap herself in before the jet took off, on its way to deliver them to a secret location for the most top-secret night of the year.

CHAPTER 14

The Annual Spy
Awards Night

As the Invisible Jet skimmed silently through the skies of England, making its way to the secret awards night location, Steinberger, back to his usual self now that Frond had gone, began explaining to Max, Linden, and Ella what their duties would be.

*Finally,* Max thought, *my life is really about to begin.*

But when he'd finished, all he'd spoken about was basic food preparation and cleaning.

"That's it?" asked Max, not trying at all to hide her worsening mood.

"No, there's one more thing," Steinberger added. "You'll need to take the garbage from your kitchen to Landing Dock Seven when the night is over."

Max sat back in her seat wondering when this nightmare was going to end.

"Look out your windows," Irene breathed excitedly.

Max was thinking so hard about the spy adventures she could be having, she didn't hear Irene's invitation. Steinberger leaned over to her.

"I think you'll want to see this."

Max turned her head reluctantly and saw why Irene was so excited. Out of what looked like wisps of floating orange cotton, the gradual outline of a mountainous island appeared. It was tall and craggy and licked by the blue-black waves of a full moon. Half alienlike, half Earthlike, it rose out of a seemingly endless sea. For a moment Max wondered if they'd stayed within Earth's atmosphere. Then, looking closer at the island's outline, she saw something else. It seemed to be floating.

"Where are we?"

"Ah, this is a very special place that you won't find on any map anywhere," Steinberger said proudly.

The jet slowed down as it approached the island and the orange glow became more intense. All around them they could see spies arriving in various kinds of secret vehicles, while waiters on small flying platforms zoomed up to open doors, offer snacks and take their coats.

"This is your captaid speaking," Sleek's nasal announcement began. "We have arrived at our destidation but have beed idstwucted to hover as there's sub kide of traffic jab. The oradge haze you cad see is a force field that acts as a security systeb we deed to pass through. Idside the systeb, you will see the full force of the isladd's beauty."

"But it's beautiful already," Ella exclaimed.

"Put it this way," Steinberger said eagerly. "This is like wearing a blindfold compared to what you are about to see."

Suddenly the white gnarly teeth and saliva of an enormous Alsatian appeared at Max's window.

"Aaaahhh!"

The dog barked back as a security officer on a hovering platform pulled its heavy chain toward her before flashing her light into Max's window.

"Security is going to be very strict," Steinberger

explained. "The elite of the world's intelligence agencies will be here tonight and no chances can be taken."

"Attentiod paddengers. We are cleared for edtradce add will begid our descedt shortly."

"I think that means we're coming in to land." Steinberger interpreted Sleek's flu-filled speech.

As the jet entered the frosted field, they were enveloped by a pulsing orange glow. Then, without warning, they were flung through the force field so fast it seemed like a g-force ride at an amusement park. Max, Linden, and Ella screamed.

"Sorry," Steinberger muttered. "I should have warned you about that. It was actually stronger than I thought."

Now that they were through the force field, the whole island appeared before them as a medieval English fortress. Except for the strange vehicles and glamorous evening wear of the guests, it seemed as though they'd been transported back in time. There were mountains, forests, lakes, turrets, and bridges, all surrounded by a commanding stone wall. Craggy cliffs and deserted beaches ringed the island and ancient churches and palaces nestled below hills. Dominating it all, in the center of the island was a majestic castle cradled by a deep green moat.

"That's where our celebrations will be," Steinberger gasped reverently.

The jet landed in a large field lit by small fires. They

parked beside a collection of vehicles that looked like they were from a Spider-Man comic. There were single-seater choppers, glass-domed cars, stretch limo-type hovercrafts, and Green Goblin-esque jet pads.

"James Bond never had anything like those," Linden said dreamily.

Ella stared at the stone castle set against the orange-tinged sky. "It doesn't look real."

"Oh, it's real," Steinberger informed her. "Just not known. Only those people here tonight and a handful of others know anything about it. The orange force field protects it from intruders and satellite cameras and makes it totally undetectable to the naked eye."

More waiters hovered by attending to spies.

To reach the castle, the guests stepped onto a long wooden drawbridge strung with thick steel chains on either side. As they approached the entrance, the drawbridge lit up beneath them. Steinberger smiled. "Look familiar? It's the Vibratron 5000. Spy Force owns the patent and very proudly export the device to over fifty countries." As he spoke, his chest puffed up so much his chin almost disappeared inside his shirt collar.

Max wasn't thinking about the Vibratron. She was finally moving among the elite of the spy world and not buried in some kitchen peeling potatoes. She stepped up to the Vibratron with her security pass ready.

A surly security guard wearing a pair of black sunglasses

studied her pass. "Sorry, Miss. You will have to use the side entrance."

"But I have a pass," Max protested.

"This pass allows you access to food areas only. Please step aside," he said as if he wasn't ruining her life.

Max moved away as other spies were allowed through.

Irene placed her hand on Max's shoulder. "Come on, Max dear. We've got work to do."

Steinberger said his good-byes and went to check on Spy Force seating arrangements. "Good luck, team. I know you'll do Spy Force very proud."

*Proud?* thought Max as they made their way through a small wooden doorway followed by trolleys of crates. *What's there to be proud of when all we're going to do is chop carrots and carry trays of frogs and fish eggs?*

The kitchen was like a large underground cave made of huge blocks of stone. The floor was cobbled, and at the long stone benchtops a squadron of kitchen hands thudded and clanged as they prepared the feast. Max's eyes were drawn to a pair of solid, wooden doors fitted with round windows. She moved slowly closer, realizing it was the room of the awards night celebration.

Inside, balloonlike chandeliers hung from gold chains suspended from ancient splintery beams. Stained-glass windows rose from rich carpeted floors to a dome-shaped roof. Red velvet-covered tables with chairs like thrones sat surrounded by a ring of flaming scepters that lined the stone walls like a burning guard of honor.

Max couldn't stop staring.

That is, until Ella bumped into her with a trolley of beet and broccoli soup.

"I am so sorry." Ella watched as Max's trousers became soaked with the red and green concoction.

"It's not enough that I have to work with food, I have to wear it as well," Max sneered through clenched teeth.

The kitchen was in full flight of activity. Irene was wearing a headset and was in constant communication with the other kitchen staff around her.

"Max, we need these eggs beaten."

"Cracking eggs," Max murmured. "And I thought my day was going to get worse."

As she began cracking eggs, Max saw a moody, ill-tempered Dretch in the awards room. *What's he doing here?* she thought. *This is an awards night for spies, not maintenance guys.* Dretch scowled at everyone, made no attempt to be friendly, and looked like he hated every second. What was it with him? Why did he even bother to come? But then his beady eyes spotted Max through the windows and he glared at her as though he could chop her into cat food. She ducked out of his view.

"Dretch is up to something, I know it," she muttered.

She left her egg cracking and crept closer to the double doors, then saw he was talking to Harrison.

"Probably complaining about something," Max

groaned. As she was about to turn away, she saw Alex, but not like she'd ever seen her. Alex seemed a little uncomfortable dressed in a long red gown and her hair in ringlets. Max thought she was beautiful.

The kitchen door was flung open and Steinberger entered, sending Max sliding across the floor.

"Sorry, Max. Are you all right?"

"No. I'm having trouble remembering who replaced my life with someone's who was doomed to hard labor."

"Oh, Max, that sense of humor of yours."

"Steinberger, Alex is here." Max scurried after him.

"Yes, she came here by plane."

"An invisible jet?"

"No. Regular plane. Sometimes agents get bored with the gadgets of being spies and prefer to act like everyone else when they're off duty."

The doors crashed open behind them. Dretch entered with Harrison and pointed at Max. She shivered. The way Dretch was looking at her spelled trouble.

Dretch wrote something down on a napkin and walked over to Max and Steinberger. He showed them the napkin: "Keep working as normal. Max, be silent."

He then ran a small green gadget over Max, which lit up bright green near her pocket. He did the same with Linden and Ella, but nothing happened.

He wrote another note to Max. "Empty your pocket."

Max took out some gum, a pen, and her Spy Force

badge. Dretch placed the badge on a chopping board and, picking up a meat tenderizer, brought it slamming down onto it. He then examined it with a small gold telescope.

"Hey! That's mine. Steinberger gave it to me."

Steinberger examined the badge too. His face became serious.

"I sent you one very like it, but this one isn't it."

The badge trembled on the board like a dying bee as the news sank into the agents like sea water into a sinking ship.

"Dretch. What do you think?" If the expression on Harrison's face could be read, it would be shouting, "Red alert!"

"It's a transmitter. It must have been swapped."

"How?" Max asked, feeling guilty.

"We'll worry about that later," Harrison commanded. "For now, the entire spy industry could be at risk."

"But how did it get through security?" Linden asked.

"By using this." Dretch held up a see-through layer of what looked like cling film. "It's a special antimatter coating that kept it hidden from the security fields outside, but once broken, the transmitter could be detected by my Securicore," Dretch explained, pointing to his green gadget. "And this infrared telescope has revealed a hidden seal belonging to Blue."

No one spoke as the seriousness of the situation unfolded before them.

"We must find out what Blue is up to and stop him from infiltrating the awards ceremony tonight." Harrison's face clouded over. "But my guess is he already has. We have to act fast. Spy agencies across the world could be facing one of their most dangerous breaches ever. One that could spell the complete destruction of spy agencies throughout the world."

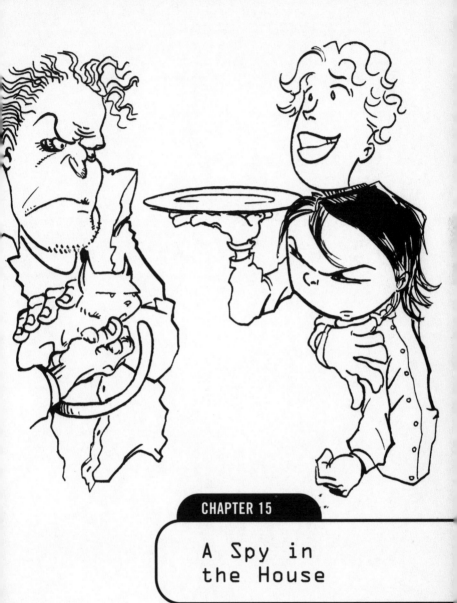

**CHAPTER 15**

A Spy in
the House

Steinberger gathered a few select agents in the kitchen. Harrison briefed them on the situation and the plans that had been put in place to find out if the awards night had been infiltrated.

Harrison then took a deep breath. "This is possibly the most dangerous threat we've had to the spy industry. Blue has the perfect situation. He's not only intercepted our latest moves on the night where every super agent in the world has gathered together, but we have no idea how he is planning to use that information. He could have planted a secret agent or a device of destruction or . . ." and here he stopped as if he was getting ready to prepare everyone for the worst, "he could be here himself."

Linden, who had been munching on one of Irene's bright yellow profiterole pastries filled with red cherry sauce, stopped mid-chew so the sauce dripped down his fingers and into a small red pool on the floor.

"Whatever he's planning, we can be certain it will be something very clever and very devastating."

The agents stood perfectly still, their expressions unchanged, their eyes focused steadfastly on their leader. Max tried to push through them to get a better view, not understanding why none of the agents recognized her. She was Max Remy, after all, only one of the youngest agents the world had ever known.

A scarf on a woman in front of her was swept back, sideswiping Max and giving her a mouthful of woolen lint. Max scowled and spat out the fluff as Harrison continued.

"One thing we can be sure of, Blue won't let the opportunity pass of trying to bring down the very foundation of the spying world."

"Absolutely right." Max was determined to be noticed, but her words fell in clumps around her like badly aimed pigeon poop. No one moved. No one said a word. Max had never felt more invisible in her life.

"This is a map of the island."

Max strained to see past a tall agent standing in front of her wearing a frilled and feathered dress that itched her nose.

Harrison outlined their plan and designated who would cover different areas of the island as Max rubbed her nose, trying not to sneeze.

"The guards in charge of the force field have been put on high alert, and the security personnel in the watch-towers are looking out for even the smallest discrepancy."

Max tried to move away from the tickling feathers but was hemmed in by agents on either side of her.

"Anything suspicious must be reported. Check every possible area for a bomb or infiltration device. But remember, you'll be operating among the best in the business and it's crucial that we keep this mission top secret and do nothing that attracts attention."

Max couldn't hold back any longer. She let out an

enormous sneeze that sent her tumbling backward into a large pot of banana and raspberry custard.

The agents turned and stared as the custard dribbled over her. No one moved to help her, including Alex, whose expression clearly said she had had enough of Max's clumsiness. The agents turned back to Harrison as he completed his instructions.

"You have my utmost confidence as the best people for the job. Good luck, and may the Force be with you."

As the agents left, Harrison and Steinberger focused on the map. Max began to wipe off her pink custard coating, and Linden and Ella made their way across the kitchen to help. Linden knew Max's pride would be hurt and he tried to cheer her up.

"Maybe they'll ask us to help," he suggested.

"Yeah," Ella added. "Maybe that's what they're working out now."

Heartened by these words, Max flicked a raspberry from her vest, scooped some custard from her sleeves and walked over to Harrison.

"What would you like me to do, sir?"

Harrison looked up from the map like he'd only just realized she was there.

"You'll be needed here in the kitchen."

That was all he said. Nothing else. He just went straight back to looking at the maps.

Max was so disheartened, she felt more gooey than the

custard dribbling down her. Not only was she not able to help, it was her fault Blue knew where they were.

Noticing her miserable face, Harrison attempted to explain further.

"Max, what has happened is not your fault. Blue will stop at nothing to get what he wants and he's wanted to bring down Spy Force for years. It's all part of a failure complex he has for not having measured up as a Spy Force agent, which he holds me personally responsible for. While the agents stop him, it is most important that you, Ella, and Linden stay here and help Irene make things appear as normal as possible. No one outside us and Spy Force must know what has happened."

Harrison then left and Max watched every chance she had of being involved in the mission leave with him.

"You heard what the man said, let's do normal like we've never done before." Irene flew straight into a business-as-usual mode while offering Max a clean cloth to wipe herself down. "Lucky I made extra custard," she joked, trying to lift Max's soggy spirits.

*Why does everything sloppy have to end up all over me? And in the most important moments of my life?* Max thought. She dreamed of the day she'd be sent on a mission that had nothing to do with food or slime or Jell-O or any other gooey stuff.

The kitchen went back to being a fast, efficient network of food preparation until the first trays were ready to be taken out. Max, Ella, and Linden entered the awards room with the tasty and unusual treats.

Max carried her tray nervously, desperate not to make any slipups as she offered it to the agents.

"Ahh, one of Irene's trays," said a guy with a toupee perched on his head like a chubby, overfed cat. "No wonder Spy Force agents do well every year. They have a good cook filling their stomachs with the best food this planet has ever had. Wish she'd come over to our team."

Max wondered if any of the agents would recognize her.

"I think it's the organic food she uses," another agent added, hardly noticing Max was even there. "I hear she insists on it."

Max flicked back her hair, trying to get their attention.

"That'd have to be a big part," another agent with a neck brace chimed in. "But she definitely has the touch of Midas when it comes to food."

All three agents nodded their heads and offered mumbled groans before falling into a reverent silence.

"Mmmmmm."

Max tried to look more conspicuous as the agents' eyes went all woozy. It was obvious they weren't thinking about her at all.

She moved away, offering her food and keeping a lookout for anything suspicious. There were a few furtive faces but mostly everything looked fine.

Until she saw Dretch.

He was standing behind a stone sculpture of a knight, talking into his coat like he was speaking into some kind of communication device. "Who's he talking to?" Max muttered as she moved behind a stone column to listen.

"Not long now and this will all be over. I promise you once this little charade is finished, you and I will be long gone and they can stay to clean up the mess."

That was it! Max *knew* Dretch was evil! She desperately wanted to tell Harrison, but after his warning last time that an agent should know all the facts before acting, she needed more proof. She moved away fast and searched for Linden.

"Irene's food has hardly any time to hit the tray before it's scooped up," Linden said as Max appeared beside him.

"Did you see Dretch?"

"How could anyone miss him? He's so cold he makes the Antarctic seem like a tropical island."

"I overheard him talking into his coat like he had some kind of concealed radio transmitter," Max informed him.

"What do you think he's doing?"

"I think he's working with Blue and the two of them are plotting together to bring this whole place crashing to its knees."

"That's pretty specific," Linden objected.

"What else could it be?"

"Maybe he's phoning his mother to tell her he arrived safely."

138

The stare Max offered Linden could not in any way be regarded as affectionate.

"Okay, maybe not his mother, but it could have been anyone. Steinberger and Harrison like Dretch and we have to be careful if we accuse him of anything."

"You're right, but this time I'm sure," Max declared.

"Sure about what?"

Max's and Linden's spines stiffened at the sound of the voice behind them. It was Dretch!

Linden quickly shuffled through his brain for an answer. "About what courses we have to bring out next."

Max's eyes settled on Dretch, who stared back at them through two unwelcoming slits, which made Linden think it was better if this meeting was cut short.

"Gotta get going. So many spies to feed."

Dretch stepped in his way and ran a bony finger through a blob of blue mash that had been left on Linden's tray.

"Just remember what you are here for." Dretch's voice had a way of slicing through them like a blizzard. "Your job is to hand out this stuff and keep your noses out of everything else."

Max's lips pursed together, fed up with all the Dretch attitude she'd had to put up with. Her mouth opened, ready to give it to him, when Linden interrupted.

"No noses. Roger that." Linden saluted and grabbing Max's arm, pulled her into the kitchen.

"Hey! What do you think you're doing?" Max complained.

"Some might call it saving our lives."

"I wasn't going to do anything terrible. I just wanted to let him know he couldn't push us around."

"That's what I was afraid of."

As they passed through the kitchen doors, they turned to see the crooked figure of Dretch as he skulked away, turning his nose up at other trays of food being offered to him.

"If that guy was any more mean, they'd have to close him down and declare him a health hazard." Linden sighed. And just then they saw him open his coat to reveal a snuggly concealed Delilah. "I guess it wasn't a transmitter after all."

Max wasn't fazed. She knew he was no good and she was going to prove it. "If he has any idea what's good for him, he'll stay out of my way," she said menacingly.

Being in the presence of Dretch gave Linden a bad feeling too, but unlike Max, he thought it would be better to avoid Dretch every chance they got.

"Or we could stay out of his," he suggested, hoping Max would agree.

"He got away at the end of our last mission by claiming he was innocent, when I know he wasn't, but next time I'll make sure he won't get off so easily."

PICKLED ONIONS

**CHAPTER 16**

Traitors in
Venice and Clumsy
Double-crossers

**Chronicles of Spy Force:**

Max Remy sank down into the long narrow gondola as it made its way through the winding canals of Venice. She'd been following the sinister Lord Luxor through the watery city for a week, secretly tailing his every move. Max knew he was no good—anyone who wore a long coat and a pencil-thin mustache like that in the twenty-first century couldn't be—but it was up to her to prove it.

Suddenly the gondolier steering Luxor's boat swung down a small waterway covered by the dark shadows of ominous-looking storehouses. Max had to be careful. She couldn't be found out now, not when she was so close to discovering the truth. She paid her gondolier and stepped ashore, where she stealthily crept along the old pathways in the direction Luxor was headed.

Max hid behind a large barrel of olives as Luxor's gondola steered into a dock and he disembarked. Looking furtively around him, he entered a building marked for demolition. With only a few seconds before the door wheezed closed, Max slipped through and watched the next few terrible moments unfold.

Luxor was, as she suspected, head of a major operation planning to hold the world for ransom and now she knew how. In the center of the storehouse was a giant machine that, when pointed at the sun, acted as a magnifying glass that would heat Earth's surface, making the oceans rise and spelling doom for the beautiful city of

Venice, which would slip quietly into watery oblivion.

It had taken a long time, but she had him now and he wasn't going to get away. But what happened next made her determined resolve falter. Lord Luxor stood before his henchmen and, with a deft flick of his wrist, pulled away a latex mask and revealed his true identity. It was Dretch! A Spy Force member, with access to all the intelligence needed to carry out his devastating plan. So that's how he did it. Max reached for her radio to call for support, when a thick-necked man grabbed it from her and stamped on it like a helpless bug.

"Uh-uh, Ms. Remy. We've got other plans for you."

He dragged her in front of Dretch who showed no mercy in his order.

"Put her in the compactor."

The compactor! Max was dragged to the giant metal-crushing machine. What could she do? She had to escape before she became a human pancake, before Dretch could have his malevolent way, before the whole world was . . .

"Max, if it's not too inconvenient for you, I'd like you to join us."

Irene was standing with Linden and Ella, and by the look on their faces they'd been trying to attract her attention for a while.

"Sure," Max said, hoping she hadn't done anything embarrassing while she was daydreaming.

"I need you all to go downstairs and get some things from the storeroom."

Max's head was alive with all sorts of special potions they'd have to find, like sleep-inducing powders or even poisons for when they found Blue.

"What kinds of things?" She was ready for anything.

"Herbs and spices, mainly."

Max could almost hear the thud of her hopes of being part of a real spy mission crash around her.

"Herbs and spices?"

"Yes. But not just any herbs and spices," Irene added importantly.

*This was where it would get interesting,* Max thought as she saw herself delicately carrying back exploding thyme leaves or strangulating stinging nettles.

Irene continued as if she was about to tell them an important secret.

"Superconcentrate organic herbs and spices. They make all the difference between a good dish and a great one."

"Oh, real herbs and spices."

"Go through that door and keep walking until you reach a round room. There you'll find someone who will tell you where you can find everything you need. And with Blue being a little more informed about us than we'd like, you better take your packs."

Ella and Linden excitedly fixed their packs as Max dragged herself across the kitchen to hers.

"Don't forget they are bottomless bags, so you can carry everything back in them. And take this so you don't get hungry." Irene gave them each a small fruit pastry and a wink before adjusting her microphone and moving into the heart of her kitchen.

"Okay, people. Let's create taste sensations! We've got a lot of hungry spies out there."

There was an increased hustle of chefs and kitchen hands as Max left her pastry and grabbed her pack. She was too nervous to eat and wanted to be on alert for anything that might lead them to Blue.

They headed through a small stone archway into a narrow corridor lit by candles nestled in rocky alcoves. As they walked, Max thought about Alex and wished she was with her now. They'd make a good team, she was sure of it. She remembered Alex's brave feats from the *The Guide to Spy Force Missions*. Chasing bad guys on ice floes in Norway, diverting speeding trains in Russia, defeating villains on camels in deserts . . .

"How does she do it?" she wondered out loud.

Linden finished the last of his pastry. "Not sure, but she's good."

"I guess it just comes naturally," Ella added.

"She must have trained really hard." Max thought

back to her own dismal training sessions and knew she had a long way to go.

"Yeah, training."

Linden imagined Irene cooking with some of the world's best chefs, while Max's head was full of images of Alex swinging from suspension bridges, climbing buildings with extra-grip gloves, and being lowered into pits of snakes.

"Yep, Irene sure is one of the best." Linden sighed, wiping a blob of custard from his cheek.

"Irene?" Max wasn't sure what he was talking about.

"Yeah. Have you ever seen anyone so talented when it comes to food?" Ella added.

"We're in the middle of possibly the most dangerous time for Spy Force and you two are talking about food?"

Linden and Ella realized perhaps Max hadn't been talking about Irene.

"Who were you talking about?" Linden's puzzled face did nothing to improve Max's bad mood.

"Alex, of course."

"Oh yeah. Alex is great too."

If this was a test of her patience, Max thought, it had better end soon because she was in big danger of failing.

They came across the round room where Irene said their contact would be. Apart from a few barrels, Max thought it looked like an ancient torture chamber. Thick bars covered thin slits of windows and chains with metal rings hung from every wall.

"This is the place, but I can't see anyone." Max's hands shot to her hips as her voice echoed around them, making the room even creepier.

Just then a squirt of something that smelled like vinegar burst out of one of the barrels labeled PICKLED ONIONS and splurted over Max's pants in one long stream. A voice bubbled out of the barrel.

"Aaaahhh, that's better. I've been in there for two hours and not a peep."

"Agent 31? Is that you?" Ella asked, remembering the contortionist talents of the hidden Spy Force agent.

"Well, it isn't Captain Hook." The lid of the barrel flew off, splashing even more pickle water over Max.

"Agent 31!" Ella and Linden called out. The last time they saw him was in a garbage can in a London park surrounded by soggy sandwiches and mangled banana peels.

"Irene didn't tell us it was you we were meeting," said Ella excitedly.

"Yeah. Yippee." Max's sarcasm was almost as thick as the food juices were making her trousers feel.

"How can you hold your breath so long?" Linden was amazed at how Agent 31 could fit into the pickle barrel.

"I owe that to a course in underwater yoga I did on a

small island off Malaysia and, of course, to the physical origami lessons I took for added flexibility." He shook his head, sending bits of pickled onion scooting through the air like overactive mosquitoes. "The ancient arts are mysterious and wise."

Ella was impressed. "I've read about underwater yoga."

*Of course she has,* thought Max.

"They say it's very hard."

"Once you've mastered the control of your breathing, you feel like a fish."

"What, slimy and smelly?" Max asked.

"No. Able to breathe underwater," Agent 31 answered, missing her sarcasm completely.

"Right." Max sighed.

"How long can you hold your breath?" Linden's fascination continued as the strong vinegar smell irritated Max's nose.

"The longest was in a sea chest at the bottom of the Mediterranean Sea. I was on assignment off the coast of Turkey. Down there for four days I was, before the enemy agents made an appearance."

"Four days! You're like Houdini."

"I'm related to him," Agent 31 said like it was nothing.

"You're related to Harry Houdini, the legendary master of escape?" Linden was stunned.

"Yes, he was my mother's father's second cousin twice removed. Nice guy they said he was too."

"Wow!" Ella and Linden's voices echoed like a pair of annoying seagulls.

Max fumed. The very existence of Spy Force was in danger and she was surrounded by people talking about food, yoga, and some guy who used to escape from boxes for a living. "Are you the agent we're supposed to talk to about supplies?" She tried to get them back on to the mission.

"That's me. Head of stock dispersal in the lower chambers."

He said it like it was the most important job he'd ever been given when all Max could see was an agent pickling in some vinegar with a whole lot of onions.

"What do you know about the mission?"

"Oh, the mission." Agent 31's face fell a few notches on the happy meter. A sudden burst of wind toyed with the flame of a candle. "It's just about the deadliest threat to Spy Force the organization has ever known."

"And?" Max had to know more. She was desperate to save the Force from a threat she'd helped create.

"That's all I can say." Agent 31 scooped a pickled onion skin from behind his ear and went quiet.

Max probed further. "Is there anything we should know so we don't jeopardize the mission?"

"The only thing I can say is if you see anything unusual, let another agent know immediately."

It was obvious they weren't going to get any more

information out of Agent 31. Suddenly they heard what sounded like miniature applause.

"Something must be happening upstairs." Agent 31 reached across to another barrel and slid a secret panel sideways to reveal a TV monitor.

"I didn't want to miss out on all the fun," he explained as the screen relayed the events of the awards ceremony upstairs.

All four spies leaned into the monitor, but it was Max who leaned in closest when she realized what was happening.

"And it is my great pleasure to announce our annual Lifetime Achievement Award," said the head of the Awards Committee, speaking from the main stage.

"This award goes to the agent who has, throughout his or her career, performed consistently above and beyond the call of duty. An agent of extraordinary courage, skill, and heroism."

"This is my favorite part." Agent 31 was munching excitedly on a pickled onion.

"And this year's award goes to . . ." He paused for effect as agents all around the room focused on the gold envelope in his hand. ". . . Agent Maximus Dretch from Spy Force."

There was another burst of muted applause as a spotlight picked through the crowd and found the mangled figure of Dretch. He looked like he'd just had his favorite TV show canceled. He stood up reluctantly, tugged at his coat, and dragged himself to the podium.

"What, are they crazy? How can they give it to him? What did he ever do to deserve it?" Max gasped.

They watched as the announcer read through an impressive list of achievements. There was also archival footage of Dretch's daring feats.

"I guess that should answer your question." Linden looked at the monitor as Dretch begrudgingly prepared himself to make an acceptance speech.

"I've got nothing to say except thanks to Spy Force and Harrison for being the family I never had."

Tiny clapping squeezed its way out of the small monitor. Agents stood to create a human guard of honor as Dretch made his way back to his seat.

"Maybe we were wrong about him." Linden frowned. "Maybe he's even better at covering himself than I thought. It just means I have to watch him more closely from now on."

"Yeah. Maybe he's just a lonely old man who's had some bad experiences and now finds it hard to deal with people," Ella added.

"Thanks, Oprah," Max snapped. "Next you're going to tell me all he needs is a really good cry and a hug from his mommy and he'll be a changed man."

She took out Irene's list, eager to stop talking about Dretch.

"Where do we find the supplies?" Max's head was like a chestnut on an open fire about to explode.

"Oh, right. Through this door, along to the next chamber, and down a few steps until you see a guy at a desk. He'll tell you where to find everything."

"Is he a secret agent too?"

"No. He's a student doing a little holiday work for us."

Max took her list back and headed in the direction Agent 31 indicated. "We have to keep our eyes peeled," she whispered out of the corner of her mouth. "We'll show them we're not too young for this job. We'll find out what Blue is up to before they have a chance to say . . . Linden?"

Max turned to see Linden and Ella nodding keenly and laughing with Agent 31. "Can we go?" she seethed.

"Gotta run." Linden offered Agent 31 a wry smile. "Before Max sics the humor police on us."

"Give us a hand with the lid?"

Agent 31 submerged himself into the pickles and Linden and Ella replaced the lid and then caught up with Max.

"Not interrupting anything, am I?"

"Yeah, but I'll let you make it up to me some other time." Linden took the list from Max's hands and started reciting the supplies before she had a chance to say anything.

Max frowned and followed closely behind until they came to the guy they were looking for. He was tall and skinny with two thick ginger eyebrows sitting like overfed caterpillars beneath a swirl of ginger hair. Under a long, pointed nose, he held a book that he was attempting to read through a pair of glasses that were so thick they looked like two crystal balls.

"Are you the guy—" Before Max could finish, he looked up from his book so fast he knocked his head against a large shelf above him.

"Are you okay?" Max ignored Ella's sympathy and got on with the list, eager to get out of this nowhereland.

"We're after some things for Irene."

"Oh, right. You're the kids I'm expecting."

Linden cringed as he saw Max's face blossom into a furious rosy glow. In the time he'd known her he'd learned a lot about what Max liked, and being called a kid wasn't one of them.

"Look, whatever your name is—"

"Roy." He smiled proudly and winked like he'd just been awarded the prize for the best name in the world. He could have been called Florence Nightingale for all Max cared.

"Could we just have these things?"

Roy took the list and put it so close to his face they thought he was going to eat it. Max stepped away from the desk as if standing too close risked a major brain drain. Ella moved in, keen to know more about Roy.

"Agent 31 told us you were a student. What do you study?"

"Aeronautical engineering. I want to build spy aircraft." And at that he leaned on a plastic ketchup bottle and sprayed the red oozing goop all over his shirt.

"There's my flying days over," Linden groaned softly.

Roy searched for Irene's ingredients, fumbling through shelves, drawers, and cupboards like he was trying to find his way in a blackout. Linden and Ella stood close to him, catching things as he knocked them over and packing their bags as the ingredients were found.

"There's a shortcut through those shelves there that'll take you back to the kitchen." Roy pointed to a long corridor while talking to some crates of dried chili. "It twists about a bit, you know how these old castles are, but you'll get there."

Max closed her pack and strode away, eager to have a life that was Roy-free.

"Thanks, Roy." Ella smiled.

"And good luck with the engineering," Linden added, meaning every word of it.

As Max, Linden, and Ella made their way toward Roy's alternative exit, a strange and unpleasant smile slid onto the store man's face.

"Yeah, thanks kids," he snarled as he took off his glasses to watch them move away like he could see them perfectly. He took a miniature transceiver from his pocket and pressed his fingers precisely on the tiny buttons. He spoke in a clear, firm voice, no longer sounding clumsy or confused at all.

"They're on their way, sir. You'll soon have Spy Force at your fingertips begging for mercy."

Roy looked down beside him, the sly grin on his face becoming even slimier.

"Won't be long now until we can let you go, but you may find there won't be much left to go back to."

Roy laughed. At his feet a bound and gagged secret agent let out a hollow, painful groan as Max, Linden, and Ella walked down the corridor, oblivious of the terrible fate that lay ahead.

# CHAPTER 17

## A Slimy Reunion

After marching ahead of Ella and Linden, Max stopped as the stone corridor ahead split in two.

"Great. Genius boy back there obviously forgot to let us know which one to take."

The corridors looked exactly the same, with a small statue of a boy holding a candle between them. Max stood in front of both and, with nothing to help her choose, decided on the one to the right. "I guess if it's wrong I can always come back and waste even more of my life *not* being on a spy mission," she grumbled at the statue.

Just then she thought she saw something dart away in front of her.

"Okay," she said out loud. "Don't spook yourself, Max." But as she walked along the twisting, curving corridor, a whoosh of stale wind extinguished a candle beside her.

"Great." She took out her torch and switched it on, which threw shadows everywhere, like there was a whole group of people hiding all around her.

"Where are Ella and Linden?" she asked, realizing walking on ahead might not have been her most clever idea.

A vase sitting in a small alcove suddenly fell to the floor, smashing a few feet before her.

Max stopped, her skin goosebumped with fear.

"Who's there?" she asked, not sure if she wanted an answer.

Then she caught the bright-eyed glow of a rat scuttling in her flashlight beam.

"You could have picked a better moment to go walking," Max said with relief. She stood taller and kept walking until a light up ahead showed the corridor she was in being joined by another.

As she got closer, she heard muffled voices.

Then she had a terrible thought. What if she'd taken the wrong path? What if she wasn't heading to the kitchen but straight into the malevolent arms of Blue? She wanted to call out to Linden, but if the mumblings belonged to enemy agents, she'd be handing herself over to certain doom.

*There's no need to be afraid,* Max tried to convince herself. *Remember, you're a superspy, you're the best and you're always in control.*

Suddenly, a moth flapped in front of her face and Max only just held back a window-shattering scream. She tried to catch her breath as the flapping insect jittered innocently away.

*Even if you have this annoying habit of attracting every creature in the animal kingdom.*

It was only then Max realized that if it was Blue she could be seconds away from single-handedly foiling his plans. She wanted so badly to prove to Alex and all the other agents that she wasn't just some custard-covered kid.

She put her torch in her pack and took out her Slimer.

160

She unhooked the safety catch and, with her fingers on the handle, hesitated long enough to gather as much courage as she could.

*Okay, Blue. I'm ready for you.*

She leaped into the mouth of the other corridor and sprang into the ready-for-action stance she'd seen so many times in movies. Legs splayed, arms outstretched, and the Slimer gripped firmly in both hands, ready to slime Blue to the furthest side of oblivion.

"You can't scare me!" she cried as she aimed her Slimer around looking for the enemy agent.

"We weren't trying to."

Max knew she'd had a stroke of dumb luck when she saw Linden and Ella looking back at her and frowning.

"Where have you been?" asked Ella. "We were worried you were lost."

Max stared at the caring face of Ella and knew her action stance looked silly. They must have taken the other corridor, which eventually merged with hers. She slowly changed her position to a normal one and discreetly tried to put the Slimer away.

"I was . . . having a good look around . . . um . . . to make sure Blue wasn't up to any of his old tricks."

"And the coast is clear?"

Max wasn't sure if Linden was being sarcastic or not. She eyed him warily. "All seems fine, but you know what Blue's like. He could be up to anything."

She was having trouble fitting the Slimer back in her pack.

"Do you want a hand?" Linden asked.

"I can do it myself," Max answered. Then, keen to take the attention off her, she added, "We better get back to the kitchen. Irene will be wondering where we are."

As they walked, Max continued to try to put the Slimer away. There was no noise other than the *phhht, phhht* sound of their rubber soles on the dark floor.

*Why don't they keep talking?* she thought. *They always have something to say to each other. Or they're laughing at the top of their voices. And Linden always thinks Ella's so fascinating. So interesting. So—*

"Linden has been telling me all about your school," Ella interrupted Max's thoughts.

"He has?" Max had no idea Linden and Ella talked about her when they were together.

"Yeah. That Toby sounds like a real pain," Ella sympathized.

Max was uneasy. Suddenly she wanted them to stop focusing on her.

"Um, yeah. He can be."

A bit of slime squirted onto Max's fingers as she gave the Slimer one last shove into her pack.

"Linden says he's like one of those bad smells that just won't go away."

Why was Ella still talking to her? Couldn't she see

Max wasn't comfortable with all this? She took her hands out of her pack and wiped the slime on her already slime-covered trousers.

"Hey, what's that?" Max stopped.

They'd reached a set of stairs leading down to a large candlelit chamber and in the center of the chamber was a metal plinth with three triangular shapes carved out of the top.

"I'm not sure, but it looks like some kind of metal plinth with three triangular shapes carved out of the top," Linden said, like he'd just stepped out of a detective film.

Ella's girlish giggle buzzed around them, and Linden remembered Max wasn't happy about him making jokes while they were on a mission.

"Sorry, Max. Sometimes they come out and I have no control over them."

Max led the way into the chamber, turning her back on Linden's humor.

Ella looked closer at the plinth. 'The three pieces look like they'd make a perfect fit.'

"Let's push them together and see what it does," Linden suggested.

"What if something dangerous happens?" Ella thought the place was creepy enough without starting anything else.

"We've flown in an invisible jet, traveled the skies of London in a Sleek Machine, and zipped across the room in a Personal Flying Device." Linden was feeling pretty confident, and besides, he was keen to have another Vibratron or Wall of Goodness experience. "Plus we've got our packs. We'll be ready if there's any danger."

Max didn't have a good feeling either, but agreeing with Ella was the last thing she was going to do.

"I agree with Linden. Let's try it."

They each put their hand on a third of the triangle.

"After three," Linden breathed. "One, two, three."

They slowly brought the triangle pieces together.

Nothing.

"Oh well." Linden shrugged disappointedly. "I guess it really is a metal plinth with carvings on it." But just then, everything around them started to waver, like it was dissolving. He suddenly had a bad feeling about what they'd done.

"What's happening?" Ella cried. The floor beneath them started to ripple and a swirling wind whooshed around their heads, turning the top of the room into a kind of rotor.

"Not sure," Linden replied. "But I don't think I should have had that last pastry."

The chamber walls looked like they were melting, wavering, and spinning like the inside of a giant life-sucking, upside-down tornado.

"I think it's some kind of vortex," Linden yelled above the whirring noise. "I read about them in a science magazine. By pushing the carvings together we must have created some kind of electrical charge, allowing the vortex to come to life. These things can be really powerful. Grab each other's hands."

Linden stumbled clumsily against the wind as he reached out to his friends. Ella took his hand. She then stretched out to Max but saw her being dragged away from them.

"Max! Take my hand!"

Max used all her strength to push against the force of the twirling suction, but the harder she tried, the further she was being pulled away.

Then something happened that sent a bolt of fear through all of them. Max was being lifted from the floor towards the center of the vortex.

Linden watched as she was dragged higher and higher.

"Max!"

But there was nothing he could do. Linden watched as Max became smaller and smaller until she was only a faint dot.

Then she was gone.

The wind tore at Linden and Ella as it swirled in an increasing fury around them.

"Linden!" Ella gripped his hand even tighter as the wind became stronger and stronger, but it was no use. She, too, was being dragged into the gaping mouth of the wind channel.

"Ella!" Linden shouted as their hands were torn apart and they were sucked into the epicenter of the vortex.

CHAPTER 18

The Nightmare
Vortex

When Linden woke up, he found himself in a strange, blue-clouded world. His head hurt, like he'd been at a party the night before and had stayed up too late. He stumbled as he stood up and tried to stop his head from feeling like it was spinning.

"I've had smoother rides," he said as he coaxed his feet to walk in a straight line. It felt as though he was walking on air as a blanket of marbled blue steam circled his every step. Wherever he was, it was damp and humid with the sound of dripping, like he was in some kind of underground cavern, but he couldn't see any rocky walls or ceilings, just endless wafts of steam rising against a background of darkness.

"Max? Ella?"

He brushed at the steam around him and up ahead he noticed a small blue light. His feet made their cushioned way toward it. He didn't know what to expect so he kept his Spy Force pack close.

But what he saw next would need neither a Slimer nor a Freeze Ray.

"Dad?" Out of the blue light Linden's dad walked toward him. "What are you doing here?"

His dad didn't answer.

"How did you get here? And how did you know where to find me?" Linden asked nervously.

He was worried his dad's silence was anger at how far Linden was from home without his knowledge. He knew it was going to sound strange, but he tried to tell his dad what had happened. "I know you must be angry with me, but Max and I were invited here to help out with a really important . . ." Before he could finish, Linden's dad turned away without saying a word. Now he was really worried. He never liked it when his dad went quiet. It usually meant he was unhappy with him or really sad about something, like when Linden's mom died.

"Dad?"

His dad kept walking away. Linden followed him through the blue steam until they reached what looked like the door to his dad's bedroom in Pennsylvania.

"Where are we?"

Again Linden's dad said nothing. Why was his dad here and why wouldn't he talk to him? Linden's stomach churned. He'd never seen him like this before.

Linden's father opened the door. Inside was his bedroom.

"How could this happen?"

His dad sat down on the bed and started to cough. Softly at first, then deeply like he couldn't stop.

"Dad?"

He climbed into bed, still coughing. Linden walked toward the bedroom, but before he could enter, the door slammed shut.

"Dad!" He rushed toward the door, determined to help his dad, when a rising swell of steam exploded around him.

He stretched out his hand to open the door but it landed on nothing. When the steam cleared, it was gone.

"Dad?" he said in a quiet whisper. His dad was gone. Linden collapsed into the pool of steam and sat with his knees pulled against his chest.

"Linden?"

It was Max. She made her way through the mist and sat down beside her friend, relieved at finding him after their weird experience in the vortex.

"I don't know about you, but this is the weirdest place I've ever been in. What do you think happened? And where are we? If that Blue has been messing with us, he'd better watch out, because I've had enough of being pushed around by his evil-smelling, slimy-headed ways."

Max stopped talking and realized Linden hadn't even noticed she was there.

"Linden?"

He still didn't move. She tapped him softly on the arm. When he looked up, Max knew something had happened. He seemed disoriented, like he couldn't remember who she was. His face was pale and when she looked at him closely, she noticed he was shaking.

"Linden, what's happened?"

He tried to tell her but couldn't find the words. "I saw my . . . my dad. He's sick."

Max tried to understand what he meant.

"Your dad's sick?"

Linden nodded.

"How do you know that?"

"He was here."

Max didn't know what to believe. The last few moments had been weird, but there was no way Linden's dad could have been here. Something was going on. Like they'd been transported to another world. One that didn't make any sense.

They sat in silence while Max tried to work it out. Linden's head was bowed and he was staring at his hands.

"Max?" His voice was so sad, Max could not bear it.

"Yeah?" She was scared he was going to say something terrible, like he was going away or he was sick too.

"I kept having this bad dream around the time Mom died. I'd dream that I'd come home and couldn't find Dad. Then I'd check in his bedroom and find him sick in bed. Really sick."

Max looked at Linden's fingers. They were white from being clenched so tightly.

"Max, I don't want to lose my dad."

He said it like he was suddenly facing the biggest fear of his life and no one had given him any warning or anything to help him face it. They were the saddest words Max had ever heard in her life. She remembered the time Linden told her about his mom dying of cancer. It was the most important thing anyone had ever told her. That time she didn't know what to say, but this time was different.

"Linden, your dad is going to be fine. He *is* fine." Max said it because she wanted it to be true. Linden's dad couldn't be sick. He just couldn't be.

She had to work out what was going on. It wasn't possible that Linden had seen his dad. She tried to coax him back to normal by asking about Ella.

"What about Ella? Have you seen her?"

He spoke slowly and quietly. "Not since we got separated at the entrance of the vortex."

Max stood up and adjusted her backpack, ready for action.

"We've got to find her and then we're going to find out what's going on and get out of here."

Linden sat still. Max wanted to take away every sad thought he was having.

"Linden, nothing is going to happen to your dad," she said as convincingly as she could.

He looked up and gave a faint smile, but he couldn't shake the feeling inside him that something terrible was going to happen.

"Come on, this place is creepy and Ella might need our help."

Linden slowly stood up and they made their way through the humid, steam-filled cavern.

"There she is." Max was hoping finding Ella would cheer Linden up and she was relieved the three of them were together again. But when they sat down beside her, Max saw that Ella had the same disoriented look that Linden had.

"Ella? Has something happened?"

She was quiet.

Max was starting to get spooked out.

"Ella?" Max touched her hand. Ella flinched as though she'd been burnt and looked at them with fear in her eyes, like it'd been drawn there with a dark felt marker.

"They were here again," Ella whispered.

"Who?" Linden asked as Ella's eyes were focused on her hands pulling at her shoelaces.

"The men in coats." She said it so quietly they could hardly hear her. "When I came out of the vortex, I tried to find you both, but the men in coats found me first."

"Are they still here now?" asked Max, worried that maybe they shouldn't be sitting here.

"They said they'd be back." Ella's voice faltered.

Then, suddenly, she sat upright, her head snapping around her in every direction. Max and Linden watched in confusion.

"Here they come!" Ella became agitated. "What are we going to do?" Before they could answer, her eyes ballooned open even wider. "They're here," she gasped and jumped to her feet.

Max and Linden squinted into the steamy darkness.

"Ella, what can you see?"

"The men are back," she gasped. "They're dressed in long dark coats down to their shoes and have hoods covering their faces."

"And what are they doing?" Linden squinted even harder, trying to see the men Ella was talking about.

"They're coming closer."

"What do they want?" Max saw the fear soaking through Ella like rain.

Ella's eyes glistened with dread. "They're coming to take Mom away, just like they did with Francis."

Linden saw a shiver jolt through Ella's body at what she had to say next. "And then they're coming to get me."

Ella kept staring ahead at where she could see the men in coats. Then something else really strange happened. Max and Linden could now see them too.

"When Mom and Francis left the Department of Science and New Technologies because they found out Blue was bad, men in dark coats followed them everywhere, threatening to make terrible things happen if they didn't give them information about the Time and Space Machine. I used to see them waiting outside our building every day when we got home from school. Then Francis disappeared and we knew that they'd taken him."

Max was frantically trying to work out what was going on. Where were they and why were they suddenly coming up against their greatest fears?

*Fears!* she thought. *That's it!* She whispered to Linden. "I've got it!"

"Got what?"

"I know what's going on."

"What is it?"

"Watch this." Max looked up. "Ella, what are they doing now?"

Ella took sharp, shallow breaths as she tried to describe what she was seeing.

"They're coming toward me."

Max took a deep breath and said, "Tell them they're not real."

Linden's head spun round to Max.

"That's it? That's your solution?" He was hoping for something more dynamic.

"Trust me." But even as she said it, Max crossed her fingers, hoping she was right.

"They're not real, Ella. The vortex has taken us into some kind of world where our greatest fears have come to life."

Linden frowned as he thought about what Max had said. "So that's why I saw my dad?"

"Think about it. What is the greatest fear you have?"

What she said was true. The thing Linden feared more than anything was his dad getting sick just like his mom had. "So none of this is real?"

"Not as far as I can tell. That's why we couldn't see

these men at first. They're in Ella's mind, but the more she became terrified by them, she brought them to life."

"Max? Linden? How are we going to fight them?"

Max tried again, knowing time was running out.

"Ella, you have to believe me. We don't need to fight them. They're your fears that have come to life. The only way to get rid of them is to tell them they're not real."

Ella heard Max's advice as the long dark coats swished around the shiny black shoes that brought the men closer.

"Please, Ella. Do as Max says," Linden pleaded.

There was something about the way he spoke that calmed Ella down and convinced her to do it.

"You're not real," she murmured as the men came even closer.

"Say it louder," Max ordered, worried that if Ella didn't stand up to these men, she'd be done for.

"You're not real," Ella repeated a little louder, but the men kept approaching.

"You have to mean it!" Max shouted, losing her patience. Just then, long shiny blades appeared at the end of the men's coat sleeves.

They stopped inches in front of Ella, their hot, stale breath pouring all over her.

Linden crossed his fingers. "You can do it, Ella."

At Linden's whispered encouragement, Ella straightened her shoulders and stood tall before the hooded strangers. But as she opened her mouth, ready to repel the

177

men, the *whoosh* of steel rang around them as the long shining blades slid through the air high above her head.

"Ella!" Linden shouted and tried to jump toward her, but Max grabbed him and pulled him back.

"She has to do it herself."

"But they've got swords!" Linden couldn't stand doing nothing while a friend was in danger.

"Linden, trust me."

But Max was worried too. What if she was wrong? What if Ella was in serious danger and they were sitting here watching the very last moments of her life?

One of the men leaned closer to Ella and bellowed a laugh that tore through the air like a thunderstorm. Max's stomach became a giant knot. She took a deep breath and tried one more time.

"Tell them they're not real!" she yelled as loudly as she could as Ella stood frozen, the shining blades hovering above her head like guillotines.

*Ella is done for,* Max thought, *and it's all my fault!*

**CHAPTER 19**

# The Nightmare Has Only Just Begun

"That's it. I'm going to help her." Linden had had enough of seeing Ella in danger while he sat back and did nothing.

Max boiled inside. First, because Linden didn't trust that she had the answer to the vortex and, second, because she always hated it when he seemed more interested in Ella than in her.

Only, of course, she'd never say that.

"The only way to help Ella is to get her to save herself," she snapped.

Linden didn't seem convinced, so Max tried harder. "I *know* what I'm doing."

"I know you do. Usually. It's just that my guess is, this is the first time you've been in a vortex and maybe you don't know everything there is to know about one."

What he said was true. Max was simply guessing when it came to the vortex. All she had to go on was this feeling inside her that she was right.

"Maybe we should just fight the guys off?" Linden would have done it too, even though the guys were so much bigger than them, but it would have been about the most stupid thing Max had ever seen.

"That won't work. We can't save Ella—only she can. That's the whole trick of the vortex. It's about your own fears. We've got to prove to her that these men aren't real."

Max thought hard as the men in dark coats held their shiny blades above Ella's head.

"I've got it!"

"I hope it's an improvement on your last suggestion."

Max rummaged through her bag.

Linden watched Ella's shoulders vibrating with fear. "Hurry, Max."

Then she had it. Max lifted the Slimer from her pack and aimed it at the men as they continued to stand menacingly over Ella.

"The Slimer? You don't think we need something a little more substantial against sword-wielding, psychopathic maniacs?"

"It's not for them. It's for Ella."

Now Linden really thought Max had gone nuts.

"I know you don't like her, but Ella needs our help and I don't think—"

"Linden, trust me." The way Max said it, he knew that's exactly what he needed to do.

"Please work," Max pleaded silently as she took aim. It was true that she'd never liked Ella, but she also never wanted to see anything happen to her.

"Take this!" Max pressed the trigger of the Slimer so that it blasted a long sweeping wave of purple goo into the air. Linden watched as the slime glooped past Ella and headed straight toward the men in dark coats. Only instead of sticking to them with its gluey, chewing gum–like mess, it went straight through them.

"Wow! Did you see that?" Linden blinked to check that his eyes had really seen what he thought they'd seen.

"Yep. Let's hope Ella did too." Max put the Slimer back in her pack. "You see, Ella. They're not real. The slime went straight through them!"

Ella said nothing. She shifted her feet as the hooded man closest to her waved his blade above her like a pendulum in a grandfather clock.

"Why won't she move?" Max was running out of ideas and getting frustrated.

Linden spoke quietly. "Ella, do you want to make these men go away? Forever?"

He waited until he heard her whisper, "Yes."

"Then you have to do as Max says."

*Finally someone is listening to me,* Max thought, eager to get out of wherever they were and to stop there being so much focus on Ella.

Then she did it. Ella swallowed hard and took a deep breath.

"You're not real!" She yelled it as though she'd been holding it back for a long time and was finally letting it out. "You're not real and I won't let you come back to hurt me or my mother ever again."

Max was impressed. Ella was a nice person, but she really had it in her when it came to standing up for herself.

The men in coats began to waver, like mirages in the sun. Wisps of blue steam rose from their coats and small parts of them began to disappear. A deafening and terrible shriek tore through the vortex as the men were swept up in a raging swirl like ghosts trapped in a tornado. Max and Linden held on to each other as Ella stood her ground, her clothing and curls buffeted by the tearing wind. An ear-crunching howl screeched around them as the men disintegrated in an explosive burst, leaving nothing more than tiny particles of blue dust falling all over them.

Linden was the first to speak.

"It's going to take a lot more to impress me now when I go to the movies."

Max smiled. First at Linden's joke and then because her theory was right. The men weren't real. She waited for what she thought was a well-deserved apology from Linden for doubting her.

"Isn't there something else you'd like to say?"

Linden's face rocketed into a wide, bursting grin.

"Sure is!" He jumped up and ran to Ella, throwing his arms around her in an air-sucking hug. "You did it! You were great! I knew you'd beat those overdressed phonies."

Max stared. She'd just saved their lives and yet she was the one standing by herself watching Linden hugging someone else.

"Maybe I'll just sit over here and turn into dust like those hooded guys, should I?" she muttered to herself as she stared at all the excited talking and hugging that was going on. "I might as well be the invisible woman for all anyone cares. I could disappear and no one would even notice."

Ella broke away from Linden's hug and interrupted Max's self-pity.

"You saved my life. I never could have beaten those guys without you."

Max didn't know what to say and suddenly felt uneasy that Ella was standing so close to her.

Then, without warning, something really terrible happened.

Ella gave Max a hug.

Max knew she'd complained about being ignored, but that was a million times better than being wrapped in Ella's wholesome and happy vibes. Max glared at Linden, trying to give him the signal that she needed rescuing, but he simply smiled and enjoyed every moment. Max squirmed as she tried to think of how she could make a getaway. Ella's curls tickled her nose and made it hard for her to breathe and just when she thought she was going to pass out, Ella finally let go.

"I'll never forget this," she said with a creak in her voice and a tear in her eye.

*Oh no,* Max thought, *now she's going to cry. This is enough schmaltz and Ella-closeness,* she decided. She needed to change the subject. And fast.

"We've got to find our way out of here and get back to the kitchen before Irene and the others start to worry about us."

"You're right," agreed Ella, finally straightening herself

out and, to Max's relief, gaining a little self-control.

"And before Blue does anything terrible to the awards night," Linden said.

Max's breath quickened, knowing that although they'd beaten the men in dark coats, that was nothing compared to what Blue might do if he infiltrated the island.

"Which way do we go?" Ella looked toward Max.

"It's hard to tell. Let's just start walking and keep our eyes peeled for some kind of exit. Whatever that might be."

The three spies walked across the blue steam-filled floor, each step leaving small whirlpools behind them. Linden leaned into Ella.

"You really were amazing back there."

"Thanks, Linden."

"I really mean it." Linden's voice lowered as his eyes focused on his feet. "The best."

Ella let out a small laugh and blushed. Max thought that maybe saving her hadn't been such a great idea after all.

"I never would have been able to do what you did." Linden snuck a quick look at Ella. "Facing those guys was the bravest thing I've ever seen."

Max gritted her teeth, desperate to escape this mush-ridden sludge. Her mind picked through all the things she had in her pack. Maybe she could use her Silencio on both of them. That way she'd be saving the world and herself from the ocean of emotional vomit that was building up around them. But Quimby's warning only to use Spy Force gadgets in the line of duty circled in her head like a magpie protecting its nest. She walked quickly ahead until Linden's swooning at how great Ella was became faint goo-encrusted mumblings.

"What would it take not to have to hear this sop anymore?" Max groaned.

As if in answer to her question, Ella's voice shot through from behind her.

"What was that?"

"What was what?" Max had been so drawn into her own mutterings that she hadn't seen the movement ahead that glued Linden's and Ella's feet to their steam-drenched spot.

No one answered her.

"Now they're quiet," she grumbled as she moved forward.

When she stared, Max could only just make out a billowing cloud effect, like steam churning over a massive cauldron. She crept forward toward what looked like the steam rising, then falling away as though it was pouring over the edge of a cliff.

"Maybe it's our way out of this place."

"Couldn't we wait until we find something normal, like a door?" Linden knew trying to reason with Max wasn't going to change her mind, but he thought he'd try anyway.

Max edged closer to the chasm hoping she was right. She was more than ready to get out of this place.

Ella and Linden followed cautiously behind.

"Be careful, Max." Ella didn't like how close Max was getting to the edge.

"I just want to see what's on the other side." Just as Max spoke, the floor of steam erupted around her like a killer whale surfacing from under the ocean in one giant leap. She lost her balance and flung her hands up, trying to grab on to something solid, but there was nothing except air and steam.

"Max!" Linden reached forward to grab her, but the steam had billowed up around her in a wild frenzy and Max fell over the lip of the chasm with nothing more than a small, echoing gasp.

CHAPTER 20

# The Other Side of the Chasm

Max plummeted through layers of sizzling blue steam. She fell so fast, she couldn't catch her breath to let out the volcanic fear-filled scream that was building up inside her.

Then, without warning, she slowed to a gentle, cushioned descent, like a carnival ride that goes into free fall until the very end, when it slows down to a quiet landing. Max looked around her hoping the wafts of steam would clear so she could see where she was. Smudges of blue-white haze floated past her between cloudless patches she struggled to see through. Then she realized she wasn't floating but was sitting on something. She waved the steam away and saw she was seated on a fluffy chair shaped as a cupped hand.

"Great." Max screwed her lip up to one side. "Just when I thought things couldn't get any weirder, I end up in the palm of someone's hand."

She grabbed on to the thumb of the chair and leaned over the side to see how far it was from the ground, but there was no ground, just a long, yawning pit of darkness. Max quickly stopped looking down and breathed deeply. "Mental note," she gasped to herself, "not to do that again. Linden," she remembered. "I've got to call Linden." But when she dug into her pocket, she found her palm computer was broken.

"What am I going to do now?"

Almost in answer to her question, a deep, melodious voice echoed from out of nowhere.

"You were curious about what was on the other side of the chasm. Well, here you are. How do you like it?"

"Who said that?" Max tried to hide the nervous edge that had crept into her voice. "And where are you?"

A rumbling, grisly laugh filtered through the wavering steam. The temperature had increased and sat on her skin like a layer of midday sun. She wiped a thin drop of sweat from her forehead.

"Answer me!" Part of Max was scared, but another part of her was prickling with anger.

"Of course. I don't mean to upset you. I have no qualms about letting you know who I am." The steam cleared enough so that Max could make out the feet, legs, and body of a person sitting in another hand chair opposite. "Maxine."

It was Blue!

Apart from her mother, Blue was the only other person brave enough to call her Maxine.

"It's always such a pleasure when we meet. I look forward to it so much. Shame it can't be in more pleasant circumstances, but if we ignore the disagreeable surroundings, it'll be like old times."

The steam cleared a little more and she could see his creepy face plastered with an even creepier smile.

He'd done it. Blue had infiltrated one of the most highly protected venues in the world. And he'd used her to do it.

*That's it!* Max's anger jolted a level higher at seeing Blue's smug expression. After all they'd been through, the last person she felt like dealing with was him. Just as she was getting ready to let him have it, she remembered. She was in the vortex!

This must be her turn to face her greatest fear, only she wasn't going to fall for it. She knew how the vortex worked and she was tired, hot, smelled like a garbage compactor with all the food she was wearing, and was completely over this whole nightmare freakfest.

She eyed Blue with a calm, steady glare.

"You're not real."

Nothing happened. Blue kept staring at her like he hadn't heard a thing.

"Did you hear me?" Max hated being ignored, even if the person ignoring her was only in her imagination. "I said, you're not real."

Blue sat on his hand-shaped chair, the steam now cleared, leaving him against a background of craggy stone, like they were in a cave deep beneath the castle. He tapped his fingers softly against each other, like a real person would do.

He should have disappeared by now. Max's confidence shivered. What was going on? Maybe she wasn't in the vortex after all, but some other place altogether.

"Oh, I'm real, Maxine. Very real," Blue said as he picked a piece of fluff from his knee. "A small problem with the chairs, I'm afraid. They're helium-injected hovering chairs, which are great fun, but they keep losing fuzz whenever anyone sits in them. Most annoying. Other than that, I quite like them. Don't you?"

She wasn't interested in the chairs. She wanted to let Blue know she was onto him. "I guess you think you're pretty clever creating your own vortex."

"Maxine," he began, but Max interrupted his condescending voice.

"When are you going to get it? It's Max. Not Maxine. Just Max." She gripped her chair so hard, a clump of blue fur came away in her hand.

Blue smiled, like he enjoyed provoking her temper. "You are quite right. This is a vortex, or what I affectionately call the Nightmare Vortex. I had it specially made as one of my side projects. We've watched you on monitors that are wired into its framework. The monitors track the position of those inside and observe their heart rate and level of fear. When their sense of terror reaches an unbearable level, the vortex harnesses that fear and uses it to help them slip into a deep coma that the body and mind never recover from."

Max shuddered at how much Blue enjoyed talking about his gruesome device and at how close they'd been to becoming its first victims.

"I guess that's not going to happen now," Max sneered at his smarmy ways, which seemed to have become even more smarmy since she saw him last.

"We were close with Linden and we almost had Ella," Blue said with a calmness that was unnerving. "But you came along and figured it all out."

Max kept her eyes trained on Blue. She needed now more than ever not to show him she was scared.

"Not to worry. With all you let us know via the transmitter, I'll soon have everything I want."

Max leaned forward on her chair.

"Why do I suddenly feel like I'm watching one of those afternoon soaps full of bad plots and ham actors?"

Blue laughed quietly. "You really are quite humorous, but I'm not sure if you'll be laughing so much when I tell you what's going to happen next."

The air around Max became hotter.

"Shame, though," Blue went on like he was never going to stop. "I really will miss them. For children they weren't as annoying as usual."

Max could hardly breathe for fear of what Blue meant.

"Where are Linden and Ella?"

Blue's eyes sparkled. "Why don't I show you?"

Beside Max, a small static image appeared, like on a TV screen but without the TV. She squinted to see it more clearly. Then she realized! It was Linden and Ella.

They were on a small beach. It was dark and they were nestled by the ocean on one side and rocky cliffs on the other. For a moment she was jealous. *Typical,* she thought. *I have to sit here and face the most evil mastermind in the world and Ella gets to be with Linden on a beach.* But then she saw something else. Crabs. Hundreds of them. They were marching toward Linden and Ella.

"Did you know that the coconut crab is the strongest of all species of crab and that it can break the shell of a coconut just using its powerful pincers?"

Max watched in horror as the crabs marched closer to her friends. Suddenly the image disappeared.

Blue clapped his hands together. "But they are the last of your worries right now. Besides, I thought you were getting sick of Ella. She can be tiring. And that Linden, he's got a good brain but he's always such a goody-goody. Gets to you after a while."

Max was furious. She could handle Blue putting her in danger, but not when he did it to Linden. She needed to get out of there fast and find him and Ella before anything terrible happened to them.

She plunged her hand into her pack and pulled out the first gadget she found.

"Take this!" Max aimed her Freeze Ray at Blue and blasted him. A jagged, bright silver beam cut through the air like a lightning bolt. It sizzled and cracked like ice floes breaking in the Antarctic.

When the ray stopped, Blue didn't move.

For a second.

Then he lifted his hand and moved his spider-like fingers menacingly before him.

"Now, now. That's not very friendly, Maxine, especially as I thought we were having such a lovely chat."

The Freeze Ray didn't work. But Blue was real, so what was going on?

"Actually, your little ray wasn't that unpleasant. It even tickled a little. You see, that's how I see you, Maxine. A little tickle of annoyance that must be removed. You worked out the vortex even quicker than I thought you could. But I, like you, am not one to be dissuaded by a minor setback."

Then Blue disappeared, like a computer that had suddenly lost power.

Max jerked forward in her chair and only just caught the thumb rest in time not to fall off. She gripped it tightly as she glimpsed the gaping chasm below her and struggled to pull herself back onto the chair. The Freeze Ray wasn't so lucky and tumbled silently into the jet-black emptiness below.

"I told you not to look down," she reminded herself.

Blue's voice deepened as it reverberated around her like an annoying announcement at a supermarket. "Have you worked it out yet, Maxine?"

Max held on to the chair's thumb tightly as she tried to catch her breath. The air around her seemed even hotter and a sharp burning smell itched her nose. A bad feeling crept over her like a million crawling centipedes.

Blue then zapped back into view. Max's head swung round to see him sitting comfortably in his chair as his poisonous predictions continued.

"I hope all your spy friends are having a good time at their precious awards night because a deadly countdown has begun that will blow them and their little island resort away. And as there are no records that this island even exists, no one will ever know about it."

"What makes you think you can outwit the world's top agents?"

"Because I've already begun their destruction and they don't even know it."

This time Max was really scared.

"What are you going to do?"

"Now, Maxine, if I tell you it'll spoil all the fun of the surprise, but you might say that it's simply the forces of nature purging the world of unnecessary pests. Oh, that reminds me," and at this Blue's smile became even more creepy. "I have one more thing I'd like to show you."

On cue, a stream of orange liquid burst from a glowing pit, filling the steaming vortex like an angry geyser. Burning embers, some as big as boulders, fell past Max, spraying everywhere with the sulfurous stench of rotten eggs.

Max's chair swayed in the rush of hot air. She pushed herself as far back as she could to try to avoid the smell and scalding heat that enveloped her.

"A volcano?"

Blue's evil laugh ricocheted throughout the cavern with glee.

"Yes. Isn't that great? And now for my next and favorite part." He clicked his fingers like a cheap magician conjuring up his next trick.

A large boulder rolled aside to reveal a deep hidden cave. From out of the darkness, a large suspended cage moved into position above the bubbling pit of lava. Inside the cage, bound tightly to a pole in the center, was Alex Crane.

"Alex!"

"Yes, it's your cherished Alex Crane, the world's greatest superspy. Only in a short while, she's going to become the world's biggest French fry."

Another blast of hot sulfurous air and lava burst from the glowing pit. Max flinched as a speck of burning liquid splattered on her arm. She tried to work out what to do. Where were Linden and Ella? What was happening at the Spy Awards Night? And what was the deadly countdown Blue had begun to destroy it?

Max had never felt so helpless in her life, but she knew she had to act. And her first step was to figure out how to save Alex.

CHAPTER 21

The Edge
of Oblivion

Blue's static form crackled as another explosive burst spewed upward from the burning pit of lava and only just missed Alex's cage. Max shuddered. Her mouth went dry and her body stiffened. Sweat gathered on her brow and poured down her burning cheeks. In the distance, Alex sat quiet and motionless. *How can she be so calm?* Max thought. Seeing Alex's face, she knew she had to be calm too.

"Come on, Max. If Alex can be in control while facing being turned into a giant piece of human tempura, then you can stop panicking and start thinking about what to do next."

Blue's image fizzled once more before his creepy laughter again filled the underground cave.

"That's the way my young superspy, never say die."

Max glared at him. "Are you still here?"

"Of course. I wouldn't miss this for the world."

But when Blue finished speaking, she finally realized what was going on.

"You're a hologram. That's why you keep disappearing and why my Freeze Ray went straight through you."

"Well done, Maxine. I knew you could do it. The Spectral Hologram Mark III is one of my favorite devices. Perfect for when you don't want people to know where you really are. It's also excellent for getting rid of pesky door-to-door salespeople as well."

"Why is it you always have so much to say whenever we meet?"

"The world is a fascinating place, Maxine. So much to talk about. So many plans to put into place . . . and power to be had."

Max had had enough of Blue and his smug plans and his annoying inability to stop calling her Maxine.

"So you're an ideas man? Ever thought of going into politics?"

"I used to be in it, remember, but you can't trust anyone in politics."

"Including you?"

Blue lowered his head and fixed her with menacing eyes. "You don't know as much as you think you do."

"What I do know is that you're a rotten piece of work with no better aim than to look after yourself even if it means ruining the lives of others."

The lava pit spewed so high it sizzled against the bottom of Alex's cage.

Blue smiled widely, enjoying Max's escalating temper.

"You're good at speeches but not so good at facts. When I was at the Force, I was the most loyal and selfless agent they could have found."

"Is this going to take long? I've got somewhere I need to be." Max was losing patience with Blue's rambling.

Blue smiled. He wasn't going to be put off by Max's sarcasm. "Harrison, for all that he is revered at the Force, is just as hungry for power as I am."

"He is the best leader they've ever had."

"Even when he almost caused the death of one of his best agents?"

Max felt like a mini-elephant had sat on her chest and squeezed all the air out of her.

"You didn't know that, did you? There's a lot you don't know about your beloved Spy Force. They may be up there now laughing and celebrating their awards but there is a darker side to everyone, even the good guys."

Max felt her chest rise and fall as the stifling heat covered her like a prickly woolen jacket. She wanted to yell at Blue to be quiet. It was true he knew more about the agency than she did, but she refused to believe Harrison wasn't good.

"Why should I believe a word you say? You're a thief and a criminal and you lied to Ben and Francis and almost broke them apart for good."

Blue's eyelids closed slightly. "Because what I have to say is true. Every word of it. Isn't it, Ms. Crane?"

Blue looked across to Alex and offered her a gentle smile. Alex wasn't biting. She stayed where she was, perfectly still.

"You're stubborn things, you girls, aren't you? Once you get your mind set on something, you just won't let it go. Still, where was I? Oh yes. Harrison. He and I used to be partners, as you well know, but he threw that away to partner with Dretch."

"Dretch?" Max flinched. Something that happened a lot whenever she heard that name.

"Yes. Dretch. To see him in action was to see a true master at work."

"So everyone keeps telling me." Max slumped, annoyed with all the Dretch adoration she'd had to put up with tonight.

"Harrison wanted the best partner so he could have all the glory for himself."

"Maybe he wanted a new partner because you were no good."

Blue's voice exploded as the lava below her surged into the cavern with a violent force. "And maybe it was because Harrison was jealous and couldn't stand anyone being better than him."

"Yeah, right. The head of Spy Force jealous of you?"

"Maxine, you're a very bright girl. Be careful what you believe. Not everyone is simply a good person or a bad person. Otherwise the world would be a very simple place. And simple it is not."

There was an almost caring edge in Blue's voice that made Max feel more uneasy than his anger did.

"During a mission Harrison and Dretch were on, they came to a point where a decision had to be made about their next move. Harrison chose the more risky route, whereas Dretch opted for the more certain road. Dretch tried to make Harrison see sense, but the more he tried, the angrier Harrison became. You see, no one argues with Harrison," Blue said with particular venom. "He decided his opinion was more important, and Dretch, loyal to Harrison, followed him. To his great detriment."

"Is that when he got the scar?" Max remembered the deep mark that ran across Dretch's face and neck.

"And a whole lot more."

Blue smiled as he could see he almost had Max. But she wasn't quite won over yet.

"Nothing more to say, Blue? What's wrong? Did you fire your speechwriter before they finished?"

"Be careful, Maxine, or sometime soon you may find that little mouth of yours has gone too far and the consequences will be deadly. Now you will have to excuse me. I really must be getting back upstairs to supervise the end of spy agencies the world over." And with that he disappeared in a spluttering zap.

Blue's words sounded like a warning bell. They rang in Max's head like a terrifying prediction of the future.

"Alex!" she yelled above another blistering inferno blast. "What should we do?"

Max's words brought the superspy to life. "I don't want you to use the Personal Flying Device yet, as it may not be able to withstand long periods of exposure to this heat, but you can use your chair."

"My chair?" Max was worried the heat had affected Alex's brain.

"Yes, I've seen ones like it before. There should be a hidden control panel somewhere near the armrests."

Max examined the chair until she felt a hard panel. She tugged at the fur on the thumb and found that it lifted up easily.

"Got it!"

"Press the start button and slowly move the chair forward by pressing down on the directional pad."

Max nestled herself firmly into the chair and did what she was instructed to do. After a small jolt the chair took off and sailed toward Alex.

*This is much better than the Personal Flying Device,* Max thought as she remembered her attempts at flying with the motorized menace.

"You'll find a release valve on the side of this cage that undoes the bolt. Once I'm free, we can get back to Harrison and try to stop Blue before he blows this place to oblivion."

"What has Blue done?"

"There is a small level of volcanic activity underneath the island. We're not sure how yet, but Blue has figured out a way to artificially increase the temperature of the magma, encouraging the volcano to erupt with a cataclysmic explosion that will envelop the whole island."

Max felt another jolt reverberate through her body. She wasn't sure whether it was the chair or the possibility of being a part of modern-day Pompeii.

She carefully maneuvered the chair through the

thickening wafts of heat-drenched steam, but the closer she got to Alex, the harder Max found it to breathe. Just then, a rush of steam and chunks of lava spewed out of the crater below. Max struggled to hold onto the chair as it tumbled backward, tipping and turning, throwing her around like a bug in a windstorm.

"Aaaahhh!" The chair flew through the air and came crashing to a stop when it smacked sideways into a solid stone wall. As did Max's head.

"Ouch!"

"Max? Are you okay?" Alex struggled to see what had happened.

Apart from a small cut to her forehead and her growing anger at how she was being treated, Max was fine.

"Couldn't be better," she moaned.

"Good," said Alex, missing the sarcasm altogether. "Now try again."

Max straightened up, steadied herself and tried again, but as she got closer to Alex, a strong jet of steam from the crater pushed her away. There was no chance of getting close to the cage.

Alex thought about what they should do next.

"The ledge." Her head nodded to indicate a small platform protruding from a wall behind the cage.

Max turned the chair to face where Alex was looking. *That's not a ledge,* she thought. *It's a small piece of rock that wouldn't pass for a diving board at a baby pool.*

As Max was about to ask Alex to think of something else, a giant eruption of rocks and lava exploded from the crater striking the bottom of the cage as if in warning that there was no time to lose.

"Okay," she muttered out loud, knowing every speck of logic was telling her she was crazy.

Max steered the chair to the ledge and tried to keep it steady as she stood on the fluffy, cushioned seat. Her feet sank into the blue fur and made it hard to balance.

"Please. Let me reach it." The moment she said this, another gust of steam shot out of the crater, forcing the chair forward and Max with it.

"Aaaahhh!"

Max lurched into the air and, after a clumsy somersault with not a hint of style, she landed on both feet like a gymnast performing a perfect finish. She hardly had time to be amazed before Alex spoke.

"Good. Now all you have to do is use the Rappeller to hook onto the cage and swing your way down here to let me out."

I guess congratulations for making it to the ledge is too much to expect? Max grumbled as her fingers stretched into her pack to get the Rappeller. Just as she found it, her eyes fell on the bulging, boiling cauldron below her.

She'd looked down and as hard as she tried, she couldn't look away. Neither could she move her feet. Her fear of heights consumed her and cemented her to the ledge.

"Max? We don't have much time." Alex was feeling the rising heat of the chamber of lava and needed the young spy to act fast.

Max couldn't move. She tried with everything she had, but nothing worked. She was the only one who could save Alex, Ella, and Linden, and she couldn't move a muscle.

**CHAPTER 22**

One Giant Leap

Alex winced as the steam from the volcano rose higher and higher, prickling her nose like a small insect had been let loose inside it. But that wasn't what was annoying her most.

"Max?"

Alex looked at Max standing on the ledge with the Rappeller in front of her. Her eyes were wide and unblinking, like a human ice sculpture. It was like Max's body was there but her mind had checked out and chosen somewhere safe to go. Alex tried again.

"Max? What are you waiting for?"

Max didn't hear Alex. At training she couldn't even do a somersault without bumping into something, and now, standing on the edge of a volcano, all she could remember was holding her Rappeller close to her chest as a whirlpool of virtual rapids ran beneath her. Only this time, the lava pit below her was real. But what was also real was the possibility of never seeing Linden again. He was in danger and she had to save him, and conquering this boiling orange bubble pit below her was the first step to doing it.

She moved to the edge of the ledge.

"Come on, Max."

Max wiped another pool of sweat from her face, but as she was about to throw the Rappeller rope, she tripped and almost fell.

"Max!" Alex watched the young spy as her body tumbled through the air. Max's hands flew around her and only just managed to grab hold of a rocky bulge behind her.

Alex took a deep breath. "Max, stay calm."

*Calm?* she thought. *How exactly do I do that?*

"Max, you have to believe in yourself totally or you'll never do it. Even an ounce of doubt will send you over the edge."

"Now she tells me." But Alex's words worked. If Max let her fear take over she could kiss her spy career and everything else good-bye.

The next part happened like Max was watching a spy film and the main character looked a lot like her. She took the Rappeller and fixed the rope to the wall behind her. The Venus flytrap fibers gripped like a superspider. She then threw the device towards the cage, landing it exactly where she'd wanted. She clutched the rope and made her way toward Alex's cage as if the spewing lava and yawning chasm were no more scary than a birdbath on a hot day.

When she reached the cage, she flicked the release valve to open the door and jumped inside. She took her laser from her pack and burned through the titanium rope binding Alex's hands. Within seconds, the superspy was free.

Alex grabbed her palm computer from her secret hidden pocket.

"Prepare your PFD. It should be able to handle the heat to get us out of here. I'll check the palm computer for a way out."

Max simply stared at Alex. She'd just swung across a burning pit of lava, unlocked a cage that was holding her prisoner, and broke through titanium ropes to set her free. What was it going to take for Alex to say thank-you?

Max activated the PFD. "And then we'll save Linden and Ella?"

"There's no time."

Max was getting tired of being bossed around.

"I'm not going until you agree we'll find them first."

"If we don't stop Blue there won't be any of Linden or Ella left to save." Alex focused on her computer. "That's weird. The locator is reading that there's a black hole above here."

"That's because of the Nightmare Vortex."

"The what?"

"The Nightmare Vortex," said Max like it was no big deal. "This creepy world Blue has created that makes you face your biggest fears. Aaaahhh!" Another gooey fountain of burning lava only just missed Max's face. "We got sucked into it just after we left Roy at the supply area."

"Roy?" Alex looked worried. "Was he tall with a tuft of hair and a fuzzy long beard?"

"Not even close."

"That wasn't Roy. He must be one of Blue's." Alex said it with a ring of doom in her voice.

Max's throat seized up as another drop of sweat trickled down her nose.

"That confirms what we suspected. Blue has agents here. He also created a device that electro-magnetically activates the molecules in Earth's core to artificially heat up to such a degree as to cause a volcanic eruption on this island. The Nightmare Vortex can only exist in a state of heightened electromagnetic activity. We have to find the device and destroy it before the island explodes and us with it."

The volcano was getting more active each second, forewarning Max and Alex of what was to come.

"Ready?" yelled Max above another blast.

"Ready." Alex clung onto Max as she prepared to take off.

"Waaaaaa!" Max didn't have a natural flare when it came to the PFD, and this time was no different. The two spies wobbled through the air, dipping and swinging through smoke and hot steam, only just managing to avoid explosions of lava and ash.

"Watch out!" Alex warned.

Max was heading toward a red-hot pinnacle of rock directly in front of them.

"Pull back!" Alex yelled.

"I'm trying." Max tried to direct the flying device, but the heat and volcanic blasts were interfering with the controls and it wouldn't do what she wanted it to.

"Max!" Alex clung on to Max as the PFD spluttered through the steaming cavern, unable to gain height and taking them straight toward a burning mountain of rock.

218

**CHAPTER 23**

Giant Crabs and
a Daring Rescue

"Max, lift up!"

Max was using all her strength to fight against the jet-force streams of volcanic pressure that were taking them straight toward the giant, red-hot pinnacle. Lava shot up around them like fireworks as they neared the rock. The PFD swirled and tumbled as Max tried to gain control.

"Come on, you hunk of flying rubbish," Max seethed as she gave the lever one final yank. The PFD lifted and Max and Alex only just avoided being turned into well-fried human pancakes.

The PFD soared over the rock, past another pool of boiling, spluttering magma and with a few more awkward turns and swivels, Max directed the device to the roof of the cavern, where they only just squeezed through the narrow mouth of the underground cave. Max was pretty pleased with herself as she landed the PFD with only a few near tumbles.

They stood on a stone walkway of the castle overlooking an orange-and-black-tinged sea.

Alex unhooked herself from the device. "Remind me next time to take the bus." Then she smiled.

Max couldn't believe it. Her whole body tingled like the smile had been loaded with electricity. She was standing on the stone path smiling with Alex like two great superspies who had just escaped death. She knew now they'd be friends.

"Now let's get to Harrison."

Using the locator on her palm computer, Alex found the exact location of their chief. Together they raced down the moonlit walkways, across a stone maze of moats and bridges until they found him in a small room overlooking the awards hall, clustered with other Spy Force agents around a pool of humming computers.

"Alex, Max. What have you found out?" he asked like he wasn't even surprised to see them.

Alex calmly explained Blue's plans of using the volcano to blow up the island. Max just stared. It was as though they were chatting about what to have for dinner, not discussing the possible destruction of the island and everyone on it. Max couldn't stand all the calmness.

"And he's using the Spectral Hologram Mark III," she burst in proudly.

"So, it's what we expected." Harrison looked serious. "Blue's completed the Electro-Magnetron and is conducting the operation externally."

The door opened and Irene rushed in. She wrapped Max in an all-enveloping hug. "Oh, you're safe. I was worried sick. Are you okay?"

As Max struggled to release herself from Irene's arms, Harrison spoke into a transceiver hidden in a carnation on his suit and instructed the team back at headquarters to aim the Spy Force Electromagnetic Neutralizer at the coordinates of the island. He then gave Alex a Volcanic Coolant to lower the temperature of the volcano. "Alex, pour this into the mouth of the volcano as soon as you can. Frond says it will help cool the magma while the Neutralizer is set in place."

Alex took the coolant and left without a word.

"Hopefully we're going to be too late . . . I mean, *not* too late," Harrison said almost to himself.

Max was getting more and more annoyed. There was one thing everyone seemed to have forgotten.

"What about Linden and Ella? They're on a beach about to be eaten by giant coconut crabs."

"Coconut crabs?" Irene said knowingly. "Mean little so-and-sos when they want to be. Come with me."

Irene took Max to the kitchen, where her hands flew through the air, chopping, grating, and squeezing a mixture of herbs and roots. "When I was a kid, I used this to stun crabs when I went fishing for them with my mom. Sprinkle it all over Linden and Ella and those crabs'll be sent packing. It's like using vinegar on leeches. They hate it, but it won't do them any harm."

She could see Max was scared and leaned down close to her.

"Don't worry. Your friends will be fine once they have this."

Because Max's palm computer was broken, Irene used hers to find out the exact location of Linden and Ella. She then put the jar of anti-crab mixture in Max's pack.

"Good luck, treasure." Max felt better after Irene's

words and with slightly more grace than usual, but not much more, she flew through one of the tall stone windows of the kitchen. She soared into the night air, starting to feel confident with the PFD until something happened. She looked down.

"Aaaahhh!" She was flying high above the swirling ocean as it crashed against the cliffs. She felt dizzy at how high she was and at the prospect of plummeting to a watery doom. The PFD dipped dangerously low and her nerves slid from brave to petrified as the churning ocean came closer and closer.

"Max! We're here!" A small voice rose above the roaring waves.

"Linden?"

"We're down here."

Max could see two people on the beach below her waving and circling their arms. Linden and Ella. She snapped back into action and pulled the PFD up from its tumbling nosedive. Suddenly, Max's fear of heights disappeared. Linden was in danger and she had to save him.

Unfrazzling her nerves, she gripped the lever firmly and maneuvered the PFD through the buffeting winds toward the beach. As Max landed with a small *pfffftt* on the sand, she saw that not only had the crabs begun nipping at their clothes but the tide had come in as well and was swirling around their knees.

"Max, you're here!" Ella cried.

Linden beamed. "About time you turned up."

Max smiled, every particle of her body doing mini-somersaults in relief at finding Linden and Ella.

"I've been busy," she joked.

"Not interrupting anything, I hope."

"Yeah, but I'll let you make it up to me some other time." She grinned wickedly at Linden as she sprinkled Irene's mixture over the crabs and within seconds the oversized crustaceans dropped off Linden's and Ella's clothes like bowling balls and headed for the sea.

"Something special you whipped up in the kitchen?"

"Yeah, and I saved you some for when we get back."

Max cut through their ropes with her knife, and when they were free, they all adjusted their PFDs to ready them for takeoff.

"Did they find Blue?" Linden asked.

"Yeah, but I'll tell you all about it when we get back."

They activated their PFDs and flew into the night. Ella was a natural, of course, but as Max sailed high above the sea toward the orange glow of the force field, she felt herself finally get the hang of the device. She noticed Linden look toward her and smile. She'd saved her friend and if Harrison and Alex got there in time, Blue would have been defeated. As she soared toward the tall stone castle of the awards night celebrations, nothing else mattered.

When they arrived back in the kitchen, Irene ran up to them. "Harrison and Alex did it. The Neutralizer worked. The volcano is quiet and Blue's plans have been crushed. But come quick. There's something happening in the awards room you've got to see."

Irene hustled them out of the kitchen just in time to see Harrison accept the final award of the night: Spy Agency of the Year. They stood watching their chief proudly, knowing that intelligence agencies across the world had been saved and not one of them knew they were even in danger.

Linden looked at Max. "Next time I'm coming with you. Those crabs were no fun at all."

"Sure, if you're up to it." Max smiled.

The three spies wilted in their tall wooden chairs. Linden's and Ella's clothes were in tatters, and Max was covered in just about every foodstuff there was in the kitchen.

"I think we did it," Ella said, happy to no longer be warding off hungry crabs. But just as they thought their night was over, Irene approached them. The way her hands sat on her hips, they knew she didn't have good news.

"Think you can sit down on the job, eh? There's a lot more work to do yet and I leave a kitchen as clean as I find it. Let's go."

The kitchen was a disaster area.

"This'll take all week," Max grumbled.

"If you add a little elbow grease and cut out the lip flapping, it should only take you a few days." Irene smiled teasingly. "Now, let's go."

They started scrubbing with all the enthusiasm of sloths with a heavy dose of sleeping sickness—until Linden noticed something.

"Max?"

"Mmmm," was all she could manage as she scrubbed pots almost as big as herself.

"I think your pack's trying to tell you something."

Max's pack was moving and gurgling like there was a small animal inside.

"Make any friends in your travels?" Linden flashed a playful smile.

"Not that I want to keep." Max approached her pack that sat near the main oven. "Maybe it's one of those crabs or some weird underground volcanic creature."

Linden and Ella watched from a distance as Max stood above her wriggling pack. A bead of sweat formed on her brow as she prepared herself for whatever hitchhiking beast she might encounter.

"Here goes." She flung the pack open and just as she did, a warm glug of sticky liquid squirted over her, followed by a short, sharp *zap*.

All three were stunned, until Linden worked it out. "Your Slimer. Quimby said it might not work properly in extreme temperatures. I guess now we know what she meant." A smirk oozed onto his face.

"Don't worry, Max. I'm sure Frond will have an antidote." Ella tried to be sympathetic, but Max did look funny. She heard Linden snigger behind her as she did a lousy job of trying to cover a wayward smile.

Max stared at both of them and wondered whether it was too late to take them back to the crab-infested beach. She stood before them, plastered in the purple goo and got ready to give them both one of her best blastings, but when she ungummed her lips, nothing came out.

"Max?" Linden was waiting to be told off, but nothing happened.

"The zapping sound must have been from the Silencio," Ella said, feeling bad about Max's bad luck.

Irene came over, wondering what the hold-up was.

"Max's Slimer and her Silencio didn't like the heat and have taken it out on her . . . all over her."

Linden and Ella tried again to stop the laughter that was itching to be let loose.

"If you didn't want to do the dishes, Max, you should have just said so." Irene chuckled at her own joke, which took away any chance of self-control for Linden and Ella. All three laughed until tears covered their faces and their lungs were desperate for more air. Max's eyes darted around in her goo-struck face. She would have loved to have blown her stack over the total lack of sympathy she was getting, but she had to take every bit of it in silence.

Irene wiped her eyes and tried to catch her breath. "We need a little help over here." She summoned a few of the bigger kitchen helpers to prop the sticky agent in a corner where she had to wait until everything was scrubbed clean.

Max fumed as the sniggering helpers plunked her down and tried to detach their hands from her and the sticky goo that now coated their palms. Her mind was alive with a million things she wanted to yell at all of them, but she couldn't say any of it.

"Mr. Blue, I think you need to see this," said the black-haired lab technician seated in front of the Volcanic Seismograph Monitor.

"Have I missed it? Don't tell me I've missed it."

"Not quite, sir."

As Blue focused on the monitor, his mood slipped from victorious to menacingly black.

"Why isn't the volcano erupting?" he asked quietly and slowly, feeling like he was his own eruption about to blow.

"The Electro-Magnetron seems to be losing power, like there is some kind of force counteracting it."

Blue watched as the seismographic reading of the

secret volcanic island fell along with his chances of destroying Spy Force.

"I'll get you, Harrison." His voice was calm but dangerous, like it was laced with poison. "There are only so many times I can be outsmarted, and the next time we meet will be our last."

**CHAPTER 24**

## Mission Complete

Linden and Ella slumped in their seats as the Invisible Jet smoothly navigated the skies above the orange force field on their way back to Spy Force. Their tattered uniforms had been replaced by their own clothes and the Digital Think-Amajigs had programmed their seats into massage recline mode.

Irene and Steinberger sat behind them and in a rare moment, Steinberger was quiet. Harrison had left the island for Spy Force Headquarters as soon as the awards ceremony was over, leaving Alex in charge of finalizing the operation and ensuring the island was safe.

Harrison seemed much more relaxed now that he was in his office and had slipped from official leader to clumsy bumbler in a matter of hours. Max, however, wasn't so much "slumped" as dumped at the back of the jet, strapped in a slime-proofed crate that Sleek had made up so she wouldn't soil the upholstery. Linden and Ella oohed and aahed at the lights of the cities beneath them and spoke in excited whispers about the success of their mission, while Max wondered about the similarities between her life and a garbage can on recycling night.

Not long after, the jet decreased its speed as it entered the VART and with all the precision of the Hubble Telescope finding Mars, Sleek brought it down on its exact mark.

The intercom clicked into life.

"Ladies and gedtlemen, boys and girls, welcobe to Spy

Force. I hope you all had a pleasadt jourdey and we thak you for choosig to fly with Sleek." The disembodied, flu-affected voice was followed by a series of clicks as Ella, Linden, Steinberger, and Irene undid their belts and made their way off the jet.

Max stood in her chewy coating waiting for someone to remember she even existed.

Linden popped his head back in the plane.

"I knew there was something I forgot."

Max's mind flooded with insults, but she couldn't use any of them. Linden motioned to Steinberger and the two of them wheeled Max and her crate off the jet and up to the Vibratron 5000. "Now, Max," Steinberger reminded her, "until we get you the Slimer antidote, you're going to be very sticky so it would be advisable that you don't touch anything because you may find yourself quite attached."

The sniggers from Linden and Ella acted on Max's temper like Blue's Electro-Magnetron on the volcano. She crossed her arms against her chest, or at least she did after great chewy clumps of purple slime extended from every tug and stretch. Why was it always she who ended up in these ridiculous situations?

After Steinberger wheeled Max into the terra-cotta pot elevators, the spies stood outside Harrison's office. Linden offered to open the door. Max hated having the door opened for her, but that didn't stop him enjoying the look of annoyance on her face when she couldn't refuse.

Linden, with an overacted gesture that should have won him an Academy Award, opened the door on an expectant Harrison.

"Ah, here they are. My favorite spies back from saving the world from one of its greatest potential flosses." Harrison shook his head. "I mean, potential *losses*. Not that I don't believe in flossing. I'm actually a great believer in dental hygiene, and flossing is high on my list."

Harrison seemed much more relaxed now that he was in his office and had slipped from official leader to clumsy bumbler in a matter of about a half hour.

Steinberger had left the office and returned with supersize drinks with pieces of mango, peach, and strawberry lining the rim of the glass. Ella and Linden gripped theirs while Max once again stood there like a flag on a beach at sunset waiting for someone to notice her.

"Oh, Max. Maybe it's best if you let me do that," Linden happily obliged.

Max fumed inside her gummy coat of slime and wanted to refuse but couldn't resist the sfruity smells that were making her stomach flip over itself.

"It seems Spy Force has once again defeated the dastardly plans of Blue, and I want all three of you to know we couldn't have done it without glue . . . make that, *without you*. Not only that, we came away with quite a load of awards, including Spy Agency of the Year for the fourth year in the snow . . . I mean, *row*."

"What happened to the island?" Ella asked.

"The Electromagnetic Neutraliser worked just as Quimby built it, so that the increasingly volcanic magma settled back into the gurgling lava bath that it once was."

"And Blue?" Linden asked through a juicy slurp.

"We didn't find him. The Spectral Hologram Mark III he built is a fed pig . . . sorry, I mean, *effective*. I have Quimby working on something that can counteract it so that next time we'll know exactly where's his fish."

For the chief of a top spy agency, Linden thought Harrison was sometimes really hard to understand. "Sorry, sir?"

"I mean to say, we'll know exactly *where he is*. Oh, and Max, you'll be happy to know Quimby has identified Blue's antimatter coating around the bugging device and she is working on an antidote. It's a tough game trying to stay one step ahead of evil."

Max's desperation to ask her own questions made her look like she was constipated.

"Max? Are you okay?" Harrison looked concerned. 'Steinberger, maybe she can write it down.'

Steinberger leaped to action. He pressed a pen into her gooey hand and held out a notepad. Max pushed through the gum to write: "Alex?"

Harrison read the note. "Oh, she left, once she'd made sure the island was safe, of course. You know how she is. Never a fan of sticking around once a mission is over. And good news about your exams. You all received A's."

Ella and Linden beamed, while Max was disappointed that Alex had left without a word.

"Well, Max, we better get you fixed up. Steinberger, take her down to Frond for the antidote, will you?"

Steinberger was instantly overcome with what Max and Linden now knew as Frond-fear. His hands started shaking, his brow broke into a sweat and his words came out like they were being spewed from a blender.

"Of course . . . I'll just . . . why don't I . . . the Slimer antidote is . . . Plantorium . . ."

Harrison never quite worked out why Steinberger was such a brilliant manager but at times became positively strange.

"Better still, Max, why don't you and Linden go down and Steinberger can take Ella to Sleek." Harrison saw Ella's face fall. "He's waiting at the VART to take you home," he added gently.

Once again, Max watched as Linden looked like someone who'd just been told all his holidays had been banned for life. Why couldn't he look like that when *she* was leaving?

Linden and Ella said a brief good-bye, but if anything could be read into it, it was more like a gushy Hollywood film condensed into about five seconds.

"Bye, Max." For once Max was happy the Silencio was doing such a good job and all she could do was smile. "I owe you a lot." Max's smile dropped. Ella looked like she was going to cry. Why me? She thought. All she wanted was for Ella to be out of her life and the chewy slime to be antidoted away, not to be part of a sniveling crying fest.

"Ella?"

Phew! It was Steinberger who gently led her out of Max's life. All she had to do now was get the antidote and everything would be rosy—except when she arrived at the Plantorium, Max was wheeled into a small chrome cubicle where the antidote was sprayed on her from a million jets fixed into the walls like an allover shower. And it wasn't the kind of shower that made a person feel refreshed.

"What is that smell?" Linden debated whether holding his breath or breathing Max's new aroma would be more dangerous to his health.

"It has a fish oil base," Frond explained apologetically. "It'll wear off after a little while."

Max took her slime-free, fish-smelling body out of the cubicle, mumbled what could have been a thank-you to Frond and stomped her fishy way to the VART, where she couldn't wait to use the Time and Space Machine to go home.

**CHAPTER 25**

Good-bye

Linden packed his bag as Max sat on her bed and felt the familiar itch of missing him rise in her chest. Since arriving home, her voice had started to come back but it was small and scratchy. Her mother was convinced she had laryngitis and kept force-feeding her hot lemon drinks with chili and garlic.

"There you go, sweetie. Just a few more of these and your voice will be back sooner than you know." Her mother kissed her on the forehead and put another of the stinky potions on Max's desk. "Bye, Linden. It was lovely having you stay. I'm off to work but Ben and Francis will be here soon."

"My social life's going to be ruined forever if she keeps this up," Max whispered after she'd gone.

"Don't worry. I'll still talk to you."

"Via e-mail," Max reminded him.

"Yeah. Lucky me." Linden flashed one of his smiles that made Max feel like she was going to collapse in a droopy mess.

"I guess landing in the compost couldn't have helped either." Linden tried to cover his sniggering by leaning into his bag and packing some more socks.

Although the Time and Space Machine had been fixed, it still had some of the old hiccups. But only for her. While she struggled to remove herself from rotting banana peels, moldy oranges, and sagging lettuce, Linden, of course, had landed comfortably on Max's bed.

In moments like this, Max usually said something sharp, but this time she smiled. Linden caught her eye and laughed even more, until he fell on the bed and they were both rolling around and giggling like they were never going to stop.

Max loved having Linden around. He made everything exciting. Now that he was leaving, her house would go back to being its usual loonyland self. Linden made her life feel normal, like other kids. Suddenly she remembered Alex and sat up.

"Linden?" she croaked. "Why doesn't Alex like me?"

Linden sat up and tried to catch his breath. "Why do you think Alex doesn't like you?"

Her words came out in a gurgling rush as Max remembered the last few days.

"Because I tried really hard on this mission and during training and I know I'm not as great a spy as she is but I'm pretty good at some things and even though I was a little clumsy at it I did save her from a boiling pit of lava and helped stop Blue from blowing up the entire world's intelligence agencies but she never once said I was any good."

Linden grabbed an apple that was sitting on Max's desk next to the garlic potion and munched into it. "She does like you."

"How do you know?"

"She told me."

"What?"

Linden took another bite of the apple. "She said she was proud of you, especially when you used the Rappeller to get her out of that cage. She said it was really brave." He turned the apple in his hands and took another bite like what he'd said was just something he'd been told and not the most important information in the world.

"When did she tell you that?"

"After you'd been slimed, I took the garbage out and saw her as she was leaving."

"Why didn't you tell me before?"

Linden didn't understand why Max was looking at him with bugged-out eyes. "It didn't come up."

They sat together for a few moments without saying anything. Linden felt like he'd done something wrong but he wasn't sure what.

"Why don't people just come out and say things?" Max mumbled to herself, but she was happy Alex had finally said something nice about her.

"Yeah," agreed Linden, glad the silence was over. "Like Frond and Steinberger. If he doesn't tell her he likes her, the guy's going to explode."

"You think that's what people should do? Just say when they like someone?" Max's stomach did this kind of weird flip as she waited for his answer.

"Oh yeah," he said through another crunch of apple. "My dad's always going on about how people should say what they mean and stop beating around the bush."

"He says that?" Max's heart was thumping so hard she was sure Linden was going to hear it.

"Yeah. Don't get him started on it. He figures most people know what they want to say but never say it." Linden thought Max looked odd. "Are you okay? You look pale."

"Yeah. Fine. Good," stammered Max.

"Hope you're not getting that flu. Knocked down half of the northern hemisphere."

"It's not the flu," she croaked. Her mouth went dry and the words she wanted to say were sticking to her tongue like peanut butter. "It's something else."

This was it, Max's chance to say what she'd wanted to say for months.

"It's just that . . . that . . ."

And as if on cue, the doorbell rang.

"That'll be Ben and Francis," Linden said. Max watched her chance of telling him how she felt disappear as he ran down the stairs.

"Well, here she is. Saved the world again, I hear?" Francis smiled proudly as Max dragged herself into the lounge room.

"Not exactly." She blushed.

"Harrison reckons you did." Ben spotted a bowl of peanuts on the coffee table and started throwing them in the air and catching them in his mouth. "He also wanted to say how pleased he was with the Time and Space Machine."

"It works great, except Max might have something to say about the landings." Linden grinned.

"Yeah, sorry about that. We'll have it fixed before you ruin too many more clothes." Ben had this way of being sweet but also couldn't help enjoying a funny situation. He finished the peanuts and plunked the bowl back on the table before standing up. "Okay, Linden. Gotta go. Your dad's missed you and Eleanor's got this red-hot meal ready for us when we get back."

Linden raced upstairs for his bags. Max's head filled with images of the farm, Eleanor's food, and the party they were going to have without her.

Ben guessed the reason for her sagging.

"Now, Miss. I've got something I want to say. Your visit's overdue. I thought I told you to come back soon." He tried to look stern as he picked her up and swept her into one of his bear hugs. "And besides," he winked at Linden standing ready with his bags, "once the Time and Space Machine has been adjusted, we'll need someone to test those landings on."

Max laughed. Ben looked a little more serious. "Your room's always ready for you, you know that."

He put her down beside Francis. "See you, Max," he muttered. "Doesn't feel right when you're not there."

"Yeah," said Linden. "Just as I get used to having you around I have to say good-bye. See you for our next mission, eh?" And with a wink and one of his blinding smiles,

Linden walked out after Ben and Francis and they were gone. Max raced up to her room and waved as they packed the car.

*How come other people can do it?* Max thought. *It happens all over the world. Every day. People saying they like each other. I can save the world but I can't say a simple thing to someone I really like.*

Linden turned and waved and gave her a salute. She saluted back and laughed. They made a good team and maybe, one day, she'd even work out how to tell him so.